D0200193

*Jack had been warned about her.*

But not for the right reasons. She threatened his finely honed ability to weigh situations and make quick judgments under all kinds of pressure. He couldn't do it this time. He couldn't pin her down.

Gwen Ashcroft was a lanky, long-legged redhead with more angles than curves, who strode in as if she didn't have a care in the world. Tall, she nearly stood eye-to-eye with him, those brilliant blue eyes meeting his gaze steadily. During the seconds when he'd moved closer, deliberately crowding her, he'd felt a tightness coiling through him.

She had an exquisite earthy beauty. It came from the total package—the easy swing of her narrow hips, the sway of her hair that brushed the tops of her shoulders when she turned her head. He saw a woman who heated his blood with a simple move, a hint of a smile, a defiant spirit.

And that made him nervous. Damn nervous.

Dear Reader,

Welcome to Silhouette **Special Edition** . . . welcome to romance. Each month, Silhouette **Special Edition** publishes six novels with you in mind—stories of love and life, tales that you can identify with—romance with that little ''something special'' added in.

April has some wonderful stories in store for you. Lindsay McKenna's powerful saga that is set in Vietnam during the '60s—MOMENTS OF GLORY—concludes with *Off Limits,* Alexandra Vance and Jim McKenzie's story. And Elizabeth Bevarly returns with *Up Close,* a wonderful, witty tale that features characters you first met in her book, *Close Range* (Silhouette **Special Edition** #590).

Rounding out this month are more stories by some of your favorite authors: Celeste Hamilton, Sarah Temple, Jennifer Mikels and Phyllis Halldorson. Don't let April showers get you down. Curl up with good books—and Silhouette **Special Edition** has six!—and celebrate love Silhouette **Special Edition**-style.

In each Silhouette **Special Edition** novel, we're dedicated to bringing you the romances that you dream about—stories that will delight as well as bring a tear to the eye. And that's what Silhouette **Special Edition** is all about—special books by special authors for special readers!

I hope you enjoy this book and all of the stories to come!

Sincerely,

Tara Gavin
Senior Editor
Silhouette Books

# JENNIFER MIKELS
## A Job
## for Jack

*Silhouette Special Edition*

Published by Silhouette Books New York

**America's Publisher of Contemporary Romance**

If you purchased this book without a cover you should be aware that this book is stolen property. It was reported as "unsold and destroyed" to the publisher, and neither the author nor the publisher has received any payment for this "stripped book."

SILHOUETTE BOOKS
300 East 42nd St., New York, N.Y. 10017

A JOB FOR JACK

Copyright © 1992 by Suzanne Kuhlin

All rights reserved. Except for use in any review, the reproduction or utilization of this work in whole or in part in any form by any electronic, mechanical or other means, now known or hereafter invented, including xerography, photocopying and recording, or in any information storage or retrieval system, is forbidden without the permission of the publisher, Silhouette Books, 300 E. 42nd St., New York, N.Y. 10017

ISBN: 0-373-09735-2

First Silhouette Books printing April 1992

All the characters in this book have no existence outside the imagination of the author and have no relation whatsoever to anyone bearing the same name or names. They are not even distantly inspired by any individual known or unknown to the author, and all incidents are pure invention.

®: Trademark used under license and registered in the United States Patent and Trademark Office and in other countries.

Printed in the U.S.A.

**Books by Jennifer Mikels**

Silhouette Special Edition

*A Sporting Affair* #66
*Whirlwind* #124
*Remember the Daffodils* #478
*Double Identity* #521
*Stargazer* #574
*Freedom's Just Another Word* #623
*A Real Charmer* #694
*A Job for Jack* #735

Silhouette Romance

*Lady of the West* #462
*Maverick* #487
*Perfect Partners* #511
*The Bewitching Hour* #551

## JENNIFER MIKELS

started out an avid fan of historical novels, which eventually led her to contemporary romances, which in turn led her to try her hand at penning her own novels. She quickly found she preferred romance fiction with its happy endings to the technical writing she'd done for a public relations firm. Between writing and raising two sons, the Phoenix-based author has little time left for hobbies, though she does enjoy cross-country skiing and antique shopping with her husband.

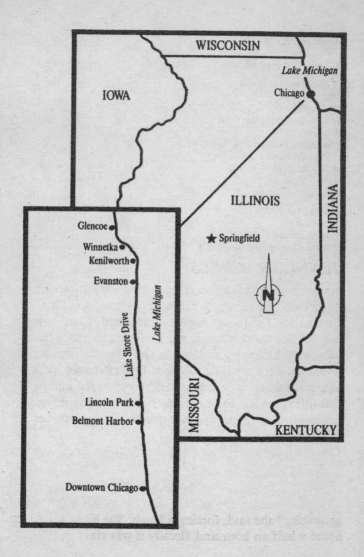

## Chapter One

"You've found me a fiancé?" They were the only words Gwen Ashcroft could manage. She wanted to laugh, but her father looked disturbingly serious. During her twenty-eight years, John Austin Ashcroft had managed to annoy her with ultimatums for as long as she could remember. But this was the first time he'd stunned her into silence.

"I see no problem." A stout man with a piercing gaze and a thinning thatch of gray hair, he circled from behind his favorite chair. "I've informed the man and he's agreeable."

"*He's* agreeable!" Gwen hunched forward on the edge of a sofa cushion. "What about me? I'm not agreeable," she said, forcing a laugh. She hadn't been home a half an hour and already it was starting. She didn't want to argue with him, but she found the discussion too unbelievable to take lightly.

Clasping his hands behind his back, he distanced himself, strolling toward the open terrace doors and the view of the flower garden that curved around the flagstone walkway. As always the grounds were immaculately landscaped. The family home, guarded by towering oaks and backed by woods, was set on several acres in a North Chicago suburb. Beyond a guest house was a tennis court. On some summer days, the chill of lake air drifted over Kenilworth and the other suburbs that lined the lakefront.

Unlike the pleasant, serene silence of the surroundings, her father's silence unnerved Gwen. "You can't be serious?" she asked, shaking her head, wanting to prod him into giving her the right response.

He waved a calming hand at her. "You're overreacting for nothing."

Nothing? she mused. He was discussing the man she was supposed to spend forever with, cuddle up to on cold nights, stand beside through years of hardship and happiness. And she was overreacting for wanting to be in on the choosing of that man? Drawing a quick breath, she considered how often she'd lost arguments in the past when she'd given in to her temper.

Moving deliberately to calm herself, she curled on the sofa again, tucking her legs beneath her. It was a submissive movement, but she planned to keep an iron firmness in her voice to match his. She knew that he would never intentionally harm her either emotionally or physically, but even the best of fathers made mistakes. "I've been away for three months," she said as calmly as she could. "And the minute I walk in the house, you give me a hug, manage a hello, and then drop this bombshell on me."

"Let's start over, shall we?" He pivoted around, an uncharacteristic uncertainty in his eyes.

What's wrong with this picture? Gwen wondered.

He was an influential man in manner and in means, the grandson of a self-made millionaire, whose law firm of Ashcroft, Hentford, and Lemas had prospered with each passing generation. And though usually quick-witted and persuasive, he cleared his throat as if straining for time to formulate what he planned to say. "You could make this easier," he urged, suddenly distracted by Gwen's younger sister appearing in the archway.

"Gwen!" Trish's voice raised with excitement as she rushed into the sitting room of the huge English Tudor home, her eyes darting from their father to Gwen. "When did you get home?"

"Minutes ago." Forcing a smile, Gwen stood and met her with a hug.

"I heard arguing," Trish whispered against her ear.

Over her sister's shoulder, Gwen watched their father slide a book out from a wall lined with leather-bound volumes.

"We'll talk later," he said without glancing back.

Gwen waited, listening for the sound of his footsteps, but she couldn't relax. She knew she'd been granted only a momentary reprieve from some ludicrous engagement plan so that she and Trish could have a quiet, private reunion.

Her fingers tight on Gwen's shoulders, Trish shook her head. "You're not arguing already, are you?"

Weariness swarmed in on Gwen at the prospect of verbal combat with him again. She'd thought their father had understood and accepted that he had one daughter who would never conform, who was more her mother's daughter than his.

"Please, don't," Trish insisted. Sunlight from the wall of windows shimmered across her blond hair.

"Relax." Gwen placed a fingertip to a corner of her sister's lips to stir a smile. Delicate and soft-looking with her peaches-and-cream complexion and large blue eyes, she had a kind heart, a generous soul, and unfortunately for her, a malleable nature.

"I want you here for my wedding, and if you two get really angry," she said worriedly, "you might leave and—"

Gwen framed her sister's face with her hands to silence her. "I won't leave. I promise." She couldn't blame Trish for being anxious. Gwen regretted the constant arguments with her father, wanted to excuse them to adolescent rebellion, but the estrangement had arisen from a deep-rooted problem. Years had passed before they'd resolved it by doing something as simple as talking—really talking and listening to each other not just fighting. It had been a painful time for both of them. It was a time in her life that Gwen wanted to forget. "I don't want to talk about me," she said, knowing her next question wouldn't ease the worry from her sister's face. "I want to talk about you. When did you decide to marry Wesley?"

Trish pulled free, averting her eyes, and nervously toyed with a brass unicorn paperweight on the massive oak desk. "A few weeks after you left for Europe."

"That was sudden. You weren't even dating him when I left."

"We've known each other awhile." Trish raised the paperweight to eye level and peered at it as if it required close study. "You'll love your bridesmaid dress," she went on with what Gwen took as false gaiety. "At first we couldn't decide between satin or—"

"Trish," she interrupted before her sister continued with more lighthearted prattle. Gwen instantly guessed that their older sister Ardelle had made the final decision about the gowns, about everything. Grabbing Trish's hand, Gwen stepped back, tugged her toward the sofa and gently urged her down to the silk, cream-colored cushion. "Why Wesley? I thought you and Fred really loved each other."

Trish thrust out her chin in youthful defiance. "Everyone thinks Wesley is perfect."

"I thought Fred was perfect for you."

"Obviously he wasn't."

Only a fool wouldn't have heard the hurt in her sister's voice. "What did he do?" Gwen asked.

"I wrote you a letter."

"Yes. You wrote that you broke up with him because of another woman." The idea still sounded ludicrous to Gwen. She had a difficult time believing that the quiet, unassertive Fred had undergone a metamorphosis and was suddenly Fred, the fancy-talking, macho ladies' man. "Are you sure we're discussing the same Fred?"

"We are." Trish pouted with displeasure, looking more like a petulant child than a nineteen-year-old on the brink of marriage. "Everyone says that Wesley is marvelous."

If Trish said "everyone" one more time, Gwen was sure she'd pop her.

"There are so many things to do before the wedding," Trish went on, in a voice still feigning brightness. "Weddings are thrilling, aren't they?"

"Thrilling." Gwen couldn't pretend happiness for her. While she believed in "happily ever after," she doubted her kid sister would find ecstasy with Wesley Bowman III. "But don't forget. After your thrilling wedding, you'll spend years of listening to good old Wesley expounding about the stock market before breakfast."

"You don't understand," Trish wailed.

"I understand the thrill," Gwen reminded her. "I've been engaged."

"But he wasn't right for you."

No, he wasn't. However, he had been the first man she'd brought home who'd received her family's approval, and the only one of her choices who'd ever seen the inside of a country club.

"Couldn't we talk about something else, like your trip? Did you enjoy France? And what about Morocco?"

Gwen wasn't surprised at the shift in conversation. Trish had a habit of ducking in advance whenever trouble appeared in her life.

"Morocco was different," Gwen answered, stepping around a bronze statue to stand by the window. A woodsy scent drifted to her with the summer breeze. "But I missed everything. I'm glad to be home."

"They were boring months while you were away."

"No one around to lead you into trouble?"

"No one around to keep me out of it."

The trace of despair in her sister's voice came through loud and clear. In her absence, Trish had lost all protection from the domination of their older sister Ardelle and her mentor, Aunt Ursula. "You were pushed into this marriage, weren't you?"

Trish wagged her head in protest, but Gwen saw uncertainty in her sister's eyes even as she insisted. "Everyone says that we're the perfect couple."

Gwen had heard similar remarks about her and Justin. "Just because everybody tells you that something or someone is right, doesn't mean it's so."

Trish offered Gwen a wan smile. "I'm reading a book on how not to be intimidated by others."

"Are you practicing on Ardelle or Aunt Ursula?"

With a mock shudder, Trish shook her head. "Never Aunt Ursula."

"She's the one behind this, isn't she?"

"Well, she made some sense. Wesley and I are compatible. Our families belong to the same country club. We have the same circle of friends," Trish said, sounding as if she were parroting Ardelle.

Gwen couldn't stifle a sarcastic response. "Don't forget your marriage would mean a merger worth millions."

"Didn't you tell me months ago that love was over-rated?"

Gwen cringed at her own bitter words after her breakup with Justin Bennett. "Let's back up," she said, leaning against one of the terrace doors. "Forget what I said before and answer one question. Do you love Wesley?"

"The most exciting thing he said to me yesterday was that his blue-chip stock had gone up," Trish admitted.

Gwen rolled her eyes. "Wonderful."

Trish fingered a fold of her flowered skirt. "Are you saying you do believe in romantic love again? You believe that the knees weaken and bells ring?"

"I plead the Fifth." How could she explain that she believed it existed for other people but not necessarily for all Ashcrofts? "I do know that I wouldn't look forward to years with a clone of Ralston," she said, referring to Ardelle's husband. Gwen couldn't recall one conversation with Ralston Van Hammon when her brother-in-law's monotone voice hadn't made her sleepy.

The click of footsteps on a gleaming dark-stained floor shot in from the foyer and silenced them both. Trish leaned forward to see who was moving about. She waited until Horton had passed by and headed toward the kitchen before resuming the conversation.

The butler's back was ironing-board straight, his manner always polite but clipped. Even if he'd heard them, he would have said nothing. John Austin Ashcroft wouldn't allow disloyalty.

"Because of father, I have to admit that I thought of postponing the wedding."

Gwen turned a puzzled look at her. "What do you mean? Is he ill?"

"Don't you know anything yet about what's been happening?"

The very impatience that Gwen had thought she had controlled vanished. "Know what?"

"It's simply awful."

"Unpleasant," their father intervened as he appeared in the archway. "Trish, isn't Wesley due to arrive for dinner?"

He had delivered similar cues to them all their lives. With an obedience Gwen had never mastered, Trish bounded from the sofa.

"Shall we talk calmly now, in civilized tones?" he asked.

Because he looked tired, she relented. "I don't want to argue or spoil this time for Trish. But my coming home doesn't mean *I* plan to accept some prearranged marriage."

"I'm afraid this time you have no choice but to do as I ask."

She believed that choice was the only thing she did have. "Why don't I?"

Frowning, he crossed the room to join her at the doors. "Because *I* have few choices," he answered rather dismally, staring at the gardens. "I'm the key witness in criminal charges against John Farrow. I learned about a cover-up through creative accounting in one of the corporations I represent. I won't go into how it's being done, except to say many people can be bought."

Gwen stepped closer, trying to see his face.

"I've received several threats."

"Threats?" She touched his arm. "You're in danger?"

He looked weary. "At first, it seemed that simple. But now the threats have extended to my family."

"Are they from Farrow?" At his nod, she felt lost in a fog of questions. "If you know he's responsible, why don't you get the police to do something about him?"

"Tangible evidence is difficult to obtain. So until the trial, we're all being protected."

"When is the trial?"

"It begins the Monday after your sister's wedding." His shoulders moved measurably as he drew a deep breath. "As I said, we have protection. I'm not sure if you noticed the overabundance of gardeners around this place."

Gwen followed the gesture of his hand toward the landscaped grounds. "I thought we were spiffing up for Trish's wedding."

He managed a token smile. "Hopefully acquaintances will believe that, too. But the police can only guard us so much from outside the house."

"Who in the family knows about this?"

"Only Trish and now you."

"Not Wesley or Ardelle or—" As he shook his head, she cut her question short.

"No. They will learn that I have a new business assistant, a rather young, thin man—Detective Lyndon—who admitted to me that he's never read the *Wall Street Journal*." Despite the attempt at humor, his expression remained serious. "And Detective Kowalski will watch over Trish. He's a rotund man who has a love affair with our cook's food. I've yet to see him not nibbling on something that Hillary is preparing." He ran a hand over the back of his neck, revealing he was tenser than he wanted her to know. "The family won't think anything of a man at the security gate. And like you, I hope they'll believe the extra men around the house are landscaping workmen."

Gwen relaxed somewhat at the idea that protection was near. "Are they FBI?"

"Police. The threats fall under the jurisdiction of our local law enforcement. However, they want to keep all the protection low-keyed, which means keeping their real identity a secret from almost everyone."

Gwen didn't fully understand the purpose behind the pretense, but at the moment her thoughts focused only on comforting him.

"I'm hoping Ardelle and Ralston don't arrive too early before the wedding, but when they do get here, they'll have a personal car and chauffeur—courtesy of the Kenilworth Police Department—unbeknownst to them. Your sister will like that." He gave her a token smile. "Ardelle has been nagging me for a personal driver ever since her first days out of the infant car seat."

Gwen nodded in agreement as she recalled Ardelle's previous complaints about having to drive her-

self somewhere because their father was using the
limousine.

"However, authorities felt all of this wasn't enough.
There had to be someone who could be with us at all
times, they said. With the forthcoming wedding, it's
necessary for all of us to attend certain social affairs.
For instance, your aunt has planned a party for Trish
one evening next week, and we couldn't refuse." He
drew a deep breath as if gathering strength. "And you
needed someone with you."

Gwen reared back. She'd been considering a chauffeur and having to give up the freedom of driving her
own car. She hadn't liked the idea one bit. But as her
father stared expectantly at her, she groaned in real-
ization. "I'm not getting a chauffeur," she said, feeling doomed to new stipulations. "I'm getting a fiancé.
But why a fiancé?"

"You've been away. People will believe you met him
in Europe. The detective who was chosen is a little
rough-edged but then so are many of today's successful men. I understand that he worked on oil rigs in
Oklahoma many years ago for a short time, so oil
seems the most logical business for him to be in. When
you talk to him, he'll explain everything. The important thing is that he can stay close to the family and no
one will question it."

She understood the need for her cooperation, but
she felt angry at being manipulated. Reason told her
it wasn't her father's fault, it was John Farrow's. But
reason was hardly enough to calm the blood boiling
within her at the thought of being baby-sat by a pis-
tol-packing fiancé.

"Your agreement is necessary, Gwen."

She nearly smiled, her father looked so beside himself, waiting for her response. "Of course, I'll cooperate."

He touched her hand in either affection or relief. Gwen wasn't sure which. "Why is it that I never know what to expect from you?"

She could have opted for sentiment—assuring him that she would never do anything to jeopardize his life. Instead she chose humor—sensing that he needed her usual wit to downplay the danger he was facing. With a shrug, she smiled, believing he needed to see it. "I can tell you what to expect: a woman's fury, if I have to pretend to be enamored with a dud, Father."

His features softened with the hint of a genuine smile before he motioned toward a man standing at the edge of the garden. "That's Detective Mallory."

His back to her, Gwen's protector was dressed in jeans and a white polo shirt. She gathered a quick impression of a physically tough man from his rangy build, broad shoulders and strong-looking arms. As his blond hair ruffled beneath the breeze, looking more tousled than messy, she noted that it brushed his collar, and a bright sun emphasized the lighter streaks running through it. She'd expected a man with hair conservatively short and a banker's gray pallor. He looked like a working man—an outdoorsman with a deep bronze tan—a man of sun, wind and water.

"Well?" her father asked.

She wondered if her father had considered what friends and associates of his would think about her bringing home a man who so obviously had never been a member of any country club. "He doesn't look as if he even knows that polo exists."

"I doubt if Detective Mallory does," her father agreed. "But then no one would expect you to choose the social-climber type."

No one would, but she had once.

"There is one more thing," he said, cutting into her thoughts. "You'll have to stay here instead of at your apartment." When she started to protest, he quickly blocked her. "It has to be this way. While several detectives are staying at the guest house, Detective Mallory has been placed in the east wing of the house."

"Near my room?"

He scowled predictably. "It's not to my liking. But Ardelle and Ralston will be here in a few days. Ardelle would expect to be in her own room in the west wing."

"Ardelle isn't going to like this." She stepped around him, an urge to run crowding her. She felt stripped of choice. For her father, she would stay; she would allow herself to be used to keep protection close to him.

"I'll tell Ardelle that I knew his father and told his son to look you up while you were in Europe."

"So all the plans are in place." She sighed and forced a step forward.

"Where are you going?"

"To meet the man of my dreams," she said with little enthusiasm.

The heavy scent of blossoms from the garden mingled and lingered in the air as she strolled the flagstone walkway toward her modern-day knight in

shining armor, but she found the flowery fragrances
too strong, too sweet at the moment—suffocating. She
was still a few feet from him when he unexpectedly
swung around as if honed in with some private radar.

His deep-set, gray eyes cut through the air with a
look far more penetrating than even her father had
ever managed. In his mid-thirties, he was handsome
in a rough way, with high cheekbones and a slightly
crooked nose. He was also more attractive than she'd
expected. What was proper at such a moment? she
wondered, doubting even Ardelle, the paragon of de-
corum in the Ashcroft family, would know the answer in this situation. "Is it Lieutenant?" she asked.

"Sergeant."

A soft haze of smoke from his cigarette filtered the
air between them, but she saw his eyes skimming over
her. The look was too cursory, done too quickly, to be
considered a leer. But the moment was proving more
difficult than she'd expected. He was an unsettling
man, the kind a woman wouldn't, *couldn't* ignore.
"I'm Gwen. The love of your life," she said, with a
soft laugh to break through the difficult first moment. "My father said you would explain everything."

He looked around for somewhere to flick his cigarette. Gwen couldn't help smiling at his annoyed expression, his fair brows knitting and etching a deep
crease between them. "There's an ashtray near the lily
pond." She directed him with her gaze.

"An ashtray outside?" he mumbled in disbelief.

She heard him utter a guttural sound of disgust before he turned away, still muttering to himself.

Amused, Gwen followed him. "There's something I don't understand. My father briefly mentioned his problem. But he didn't say more than that there had been threats. What kind of threats?"

"Phone calls," he answered simply without looking back.

Silently Gwen bristled at his answer. Did he think she was some fluff too dim-witted to realize that more had to have happened? She drilled his back with an appropriate glare, but for now she decided to let him evade her question. "What happens after the wedding?"

He paused in grinding out the cigarette and swung a puzzled look over his shoulder. "The trial starts."

Gwen jammed a hand into her skirt pocket as a touch of impatience swept through her. "I meant what kind of protection will he have?"

Straightening, he fixed intense-looking eyes on her. "We'll place your father in protective custody—what we've wanted to do from the start." He slouched lazily against a stone pillar. "But because of your sister's wedding, he refused that idea, saying he wouldn't change any of his plans. After the wedding, your sister will be on her honeymoon, so she won't be a problem."

In her peripheral vision Gwen caught a glimpse of her father standing on the terrace and watching them.

"You don't live here, do you?"

Gwen drew her attention back to him. "No, I have an apartment near the lake."

"If we have to, we'll make arrangements for you then."

She didn't want anyone making plans for her. "What kind of arrangements?"

"Like your father, you'd be placed in protective custody until there's a conviction."

A protest rose within her as she considered how long the trial might take and the numerous appeals that might follow. Unlike the rest of her family, she couldn't just place her life in a stranger's hands. "Sergeant, I realize that you have a job to do, but I don't like this bogus engagement that my father thought up."

"He didn't," he said quietly. "We did." He shoved away from the statue. "Is there a point to all of this?"

Gwen wasn't certain there was. Though she'd promised her father that she'd cooperate, she didn't want to give up complete control of her life. "I'm over twenty-one. I make my own decisions."

"Is that right?" Unexpectedly he flashed a grin, a disarmingly wry one that convinced Gwen he was used to creating disturbances among the female population. "Let's get one thing straight," he insisted, stepping closer until only inches separated them.

Gwen heard the warning in his voice. For one second—the longest second she'd ever experienced—he made no other move. She watched his gaze sweep over her face and then settle on her lips, felt the heat of his breath fanning her cheek, and self-consciously raised a hand to push back a strand of hair flying across it.

His eyes locked on hers as he blocked her hand. With a touch far lighter, far gentler than she ever expected, he tucked the hair behind her ear. "Where you go, I go."

Something fluttered within her besides nervousness. "We'll see," she answered with an uncharacteristic haughtiness that tried to mask her uncertainty.

Whirling away, she wished her legs felt as firm as her voice had been. Even her stomach somersaulted in mockery of her cool manner.

As she strolled past her father, he sent her a troubled frown. "Gwen, step carefully. He's not like any man you've ever known." He said it to her back as she walked away.

"We're in agreement," she returned, without slowing down her stride.

"He's here for one reason," he seemed to feel the need to remind her. "To keep you safe."

"Is he?" She kept on walking, aware that instead of feeling safer, she felt she'd opened a door that might lead to a very dangerous place.

Jack had been warned about her, but not for the right reasons. She threatened his finely honed ability to weigh situations and make quick judgments under all kinds of pressure. He couldn't do it this time. He couldn't pin her down.

He'd expected a blonde like the bride-to-be, but Gwen Ashcroft was a lanky, long-legged redhead with more angles than curves, who strode in a loose-limbed manner as if she didn't have a care in the world. Tall, she'd nearly stood eye-to-eye with him, those brilliant blue eyes meeting his gaze steadily. During the seconds when he'd moved closer, deliberately crowding her, he'd felt a tightness coiling through him. He doubted most men didn't feel something similar when facing her.

Though her nose was a touch too long and too pointed, she had an exquisite earthy beauty. It came from the total package—the easy swing of her narrow hips, the sway of her hair that brushed the tops of her shoulders when she turned her head. He saw a woman who heated his blood with a simple move, a hint of a smile, a defiant spirit. And that made him nervous. Damn nervous.

"Dynamite-looking lady." Earl Kowalski sidled close, grinning.

Jack didn't respond to his partner's comment. But it was clear that she'd already distracted him, otherwise Earl would never have gotten so close without Jack hearing him.

"What's she like?" Earl asked, munching on a cookie.

Jack sent him a look of disbelief. "Are you eating again? You're gonna burst."

"They got a great cook. Food is my consolation prize for not pulling your duty."

A paunchy man, a few years younger than Jack, Earl had been an MP in the Army. Police work had seemed his calling. He had a gregarious Italian wife who talked nonstop and served out-of-this-world lasagna. They had a two-year-old replica of the square-jawed Earl.

"Your wife wouldn't have liked it," Jack reminded him.

"Guess that's why you were chosen instead."

The captain had said the same thing. Unlike Earl, Jack wasn't married. He had no family responsibilities and no romantic commitments. He had an apartment near the lake, a sailboat and his job. He never dwelled on the fact that he was without ties. He'd never had them; since childhood, he had learned to stand alone.

"So what's she like?" Earl repeated.

"What you said."

Earl's cheeks bunched with his grin. "Already in love?"

"You're a damn romantic," Jack quipped, stepping away.

"Cynics die earlier." Earl lumbered over beside him. "Too much stress."

Jack smiled grudgingly and swept out his arm. "Look around you." Set back from the highway and bordered by woods, the Ashcrofts' Tudor home reminded Jack too much of Christina's home. When he'd arrived earlier, driving up the winding driveway toward the sprawling house, he had noticed the tennis courts. An avid sportsman who'd once considered a professional baseball career, he'd never even picked up a racket. The Ashcrofts' was a different world. "What would you expect? She's someone who's used to getting her way."

Earl gave him another stupid, taunting grin. "Watching out for a real looker sounds like a breezy assignment to me."

"It's still called baby-sitting."

"At least Lyndon got assigned to the old man. I'm lousy at being a yes-man." Earl pulled uncomfortably at the stiff collar of his newly acquired chauffeur's uniform. "But so far, no problems."

"Yeah. No problems," Jack mumbled. "Except the princess doesn't like this arrangement."

Snorting, Earl doffed his chauffeur's cap as he departed. "Guess that means you're not her Prince Charming."

Jack sent him a deadly look.

Laughing to himself, Earl ambled toward the garage.

As Jack wandered toward the house, he wished he could drum up amusement. His was going to be a long, hard engagement to Gwen Ashcroft. He hadn't wanted the assignment from the start, knowing it would revive too many memories of another woman who knew the privileges of a moneyed life.

Reaching the front door, he paused to survey the surroundings. Besides the sprawling mansion, there was a four-car garage and a pool house. Everything was attached to the main building by overhangs except the gate house. Because only a few oak trees bordered the drive, he and the other detectives had a clear view across the lush, landscaped lawn all the way from the house to the wrought iron fence and security gate. The back of the house offered the real security risk. Flower-lined walkways led unobstructed to a massive garden and beyond that to the woods.

The back of the house was too accessible. That bothered him. So did the quietness. He was used to the sounds of the city, the blare of horns, the buzz of people, women who liked beer and baseball games. Champagne and the symphony better suited the occupants of this house, he thought, as he stepped into a dark-stained foyer beneath a high ceiling and hand-cut crystal chandelier.

Five years seemed like such a long time now, but he could still remember walking into a palatial home similar to the Ashcrofts'. When he'd left for the last time, he had promised himself he would stay clear of any woman who lived in a house like it. He reflected on old memories, painful ones, amazed they could still haunt him.

He ambled past the family portraits of austere-looking people and into the living room with its massive stone hearth and beamed cathedral ceiling. Like the other rooms filled with expensive antiques, it was decorated more for style than comfort. Everything had style, he mused as he listened to the soft melodious chimes of the doorbell.

Stopping, he could see into a nearby sitting room. He saw the bride-to-be rush from a brocade sofa to a window and push back the heavy drapes. Even from a distance, Jack could see her skin pale.

"It's Fred," Trish Ashcroft announced with an odd combination of distress and a hint of pleasure.

"Fred?" her father parroted.

"Yes, Fred."

Jack recalled the man's full name from a sketchy briefing the detectives had been given. Frederick Gladstone, ex-boyfriend of Trish Ashcroft. Frowning, Jack whipped around as he wondered how Gladstone had managed to get past the detective dressed as a security guard at the gate.

He reached the front door in time to see Gwen, dressed in shorts, T-shirt and sneakers, heading toward the path that led into the woods.

## Chapter Two

Why was she so uptight? Gwen wondered, her feet pounding into the dirt path. In her family, she'd always been the one who took any change in stride, who searched for levity during what were disastrous moments by others' standards.

But this time was different, she thought with an honesty that was painful. It was more than the restrictions. The moment he'd flashed that damnable grin of his, she'd wanted to call off the forced relationship out of pure female fear. Reneging didn't sit well with her. She believed that a person's word should stand for something. And she had assured her father she would cooperate. But it looked like Rebellious Gwen was alive and ready to fight again, and not at all happy with herself for it. Old habits did die hard.

Wasn't that why she was running now? She needed to slip into some kind of familiar routine, keep herself from worrying too much about the danger to her father. In her usual way, she forced a bright mood on herself. As she hummed a light tune, she felt more in control of everything around her, easing the restlessness away.

The sun peeked through the trees, dashing the path with splashes of light. As her sneakered feet hit the dirt trail harder, she drew a deep breath and began to pace herself to reach the pond at the edge of the woods.

Between gnarled branches of trees, she saw the blue water shimmering beneath the sunlight. Perspiration bathed the back of her neck by the time she reached the pond. Winded, she bent over and laid her hands on her knees. As she drew several deep breaths, she listened to the familiar sounds around her, a squirrel scurrying up a tree, birds chirping, the faint rustle of leaves beneath the summer breeze.

Some sense of normalcy drifted over her. This was what she'd been seeking most of all since she'd arrived. Few knew the extent of discomfort she felt, had always felt, in the midst of her family's wealth. She had resisted the codes of affluent propriety, seeking to make her own life. She'd always blamed it on the French and Irish temperament from her mother's side of the family. But no one else understood, just as they hadn't understood why she'd ended her relationship with the only man she'd ever chosen who would have been welcomed into the family.

Sighing, Gwen shook her head, trying not to let memories of Justin intrude. Dangling her arms, she started to draw another deep breath, but a soft pounding sound drew her to stiff attention. The breath she had been trying to recapture was snatched from her. Blood pounding in her head, she stared up at Jack Mallory's angry face.

"What the hell are you doing out here?" he asked, breathing hard.

Gwen managed a small smile. "Running," she said simply.

"Dammit, stop acting like an idiot."

"Idiot?"

"You're receiving round-the-clock protection. Do you understand that?" he demanded.

"I understand that it's broad daylight, Sergeant." Gwen just barely held on to her temper. "I think I'm safe," she snapped, brushing past him and stomping forward.

Before she reached the edge of the woods, he was by her side, matching her stride, managing to engineer himself much too close to her. "I decide if you're safe."

Gwen scowled at him and kept up her clipped pace as she marched toward the back of the house and the kitchen.

Moving too quickly for her, Jack snagged her arm before she could reach the kitchen door. "I told you before. Where you go, I go."

Gwen glared down at the fingers clamped over her arm. No one manhandled her. Defiance rushed through her; she raised her face to him, narrowing her eyes dangerously.

Though his stare never wavered, he opened his fingers from their tight grip on her wrist. Lightly he ran a thumb across the spot he had held, uncertain if he'd bruised her flesh. "I'm here to protect you," he said more softly, not pleased by his unreasonable anger. He usually controlled himself better. "I'm not your enemy," he tried to reason.

Hearing a quieter tone edge his gravelly voice, Gwen tried to make her own mood more gentle. While she honestly didn't believe she'd done anything catastrophic, she could understand some of his annoyance. He had a responsibility. And he was right—*he* wasn't the enemy. So why had she acted so unyielding toward him?

She sighed heavily, annoyed at her own quick temper. She was usually calmer, more easy going. Who was she fighting? Him or years of feeling too much constraint? He has a job to do, she reminded herself. He probably dislikes just being here and she certainly wasn't making things easier for him.

She raised a hand to blot perspiration from her face. She was tenser than she realized, uptight about being home again, about a wedding that shouldn't be taking place, about a danger to her father that she didn't quite understand. And extremely uncomfortable with the man who would be protecting her. None of it was really his fault, but unfairly she'd vented all her frustration at him. Gearing up courage, she stalled to draw another deep breath. "I owe you an apology, don't I?"

Jack noted the weakening in her voice.

"Before we go in, you'd better tell me what our game plan is," she said suddenly.

He looked understandably wary. "Are you saying we're done with all the spoiled-brat antics? You're willing to cooperate?"

Gwen decided diplomacy wasn't his forte. "I have been cooperating." She gave him a weak smile. "Reluctantly." Straightening her back, she told herself she would get through this charade, but she wasn't as confident as she wanted to be. "Just be warned. I'm no actress."

He looked down at her wrist, saw the faint redness and knew his fingers hadn't been gentle. "We'll manage," he said, then reached around her to open the door.

The cook glanced up from swirling frosting on a cake. A short, ample-figured woman who barely reached Jack's chin, she possessed a steady stare that dared anyone to give her trouble at the door.

She and the butler had been servants to the Ashcrofts for nearly forty years. Gwen's father had argued that they should be privy to the family dilemma. The police stance had been firm. The fewer people who knew, the better.

Removing a pitcher from the refrigerator, Hillary approached the table, her mass of gray hair swaying in a lopsided bun atop her head. "Your lemonade is all made," she announced. "Would you like some, sir?" As Jack shook his head, she handed Gwen a glass. "I knew you'd be running as soon as you came home."

Gwen touched her shoulder affectionately. "Thank you, Hillary."

Jack considered the scenario before him with as much objectivity as he could. He was getting mixed signals. He had thought she'd entered the kitchen because it was the quickest way to evade him. He realized now that a routine existed between the cook and her. He couldn't pigeonhole Gwen Ashcroft as a spoiled, self-centered woman. Spirited, yes. Annoying, infuriating, and more, he acknowledged, as he felt a genuine warmth emanating from her to the cook.

Hillary scurried to a cabinet. "I'll get you some cookies."

Jack stayed near the door and a clear view of the garden area and the winding driveway. Outside, Earl was polishing the hood of a limousine. Jack made a mental note to razz him about it later.

He refocused on the woman standing near the refrigerator. He had to know her habits, the way she thought. He had to second-guess her to protect her properly.

"A peace offering, *darling?*" she asked as she set the plate of cookies on the table near him. The endearment had come out as if it had been stuck in her throat.

Jack sensed how difficult it was for her to pretend something she didn't feel. That surprised him. Game playing had been Christina's specialty.

Beaming, delighted at the romance buzzing around her, Hillary turned away to resume swirling chocolate frosting on the cake.

With their audience of one preoccupied, Gwen relaxed slightly. She turned away from him and took several sips of the lemonade. It was tart to match her mood. She hated the whole situation, she realized, truly hated having other people tell her what to do. And how much would this man, whom she wasn't even sure she liked, expect her to pretend with him?

She noted that he finally had moved away from the door to take one of Hillary's cookies. For some reason, she felt a slip of reassurance in learning that he couldn't resist them any more than she could. She forced a lightness to her voice for Hillary. If she wasn't careful, this woman, who'd listened to her youthful tales of school and boyfriends, would see right through their pretense. "Hillary, will you make the dinner I requested?"

Hillary shot back a frown of disapproval over her shoulder. "Mr. Bowman is coming tonight."

"Then that's all the more reason to serve it," she said to stir the woman's amusement.

"What are you up to?" he questioned Gwen, in the manner of a concerned fiancé.

"What's expected."

It wasn't a statement of pride, just fact, Jack noted.

"In time, you'll see that what I've told you is true."

He wondered what it was he was supposed to know.

"As I said before," she explained calmly. She seemed to be getting over some of her uneasiness about their mock relationship. "I'm good grist for the mill. Every article ever written about the family has managed to include something about me that's aroused family unrest."

"There's nothing wrong with you," Hillary piped in defensively. "Except for a little devilment."

"She's dear, isn't she?" Gwen sent her a thank-you smile. "But really, I'm the oddball sister." She strolled closer to Hillary and stared at the bowl of frosting. "I don't relish being tagged as the family embarrassment. At least I'm invited to the wedding." She swiped a finger at the frosting. "Uncle Waldo won't be."

Jack had been briefed on people who knew the Ashcrofts. To his advantage, he had an almost photographic memory. Waldo LeClare was her mother's brother and not of the Ashcroft bloodline.

"Can you imagine?" she asked, sounding more miffed than surprised. "Five hundred guests but they couldn't include him."

He heard her irritation, saw it in the tense line of her mouth.

"He was excluded on purpose," she whispered, though only the loyal Hillary was in hearing distance. "No one cares if he knows that he's viewed as an outcast." Glancing at him, Gwen noticed he wasn't looking at her but toward the car that had just arrived. "Wesley." She couldn't keep the disgust out of her voice. "That's the groom-to-be."

Jack eyed the gray Mercedes while taking a bite of cookie. "Wesley Bowman?"

"Wesley Bowman III," she corrected mockingly.

The man getting out of the car was of average height with a short brown military haircut. He wore a light gray, three-piece suit. He had the kind of average-looking face that would be tough to pick out in a crowd, Jack noted.

"Ralston, my other sister Ardelle's husband—" She paused, as if letting her explanation of the family connection seep in. "He's a second cousin to Wesley. They introduced Wesley to Trish years ago and have been browbeating her into a relationship with him ever since. He'll blend nicely. That's what pleases them."

Jack was suddenly certain that she had never blended.

She glanced back out the window at the car. "I should go. I can imagine what Trish is doing with Fred and Wesley in the same room. She really should have been born on a plantation before the Civil War. She's mastered swooning."

He saw a sparkle of humor in her eyes. They were the first thing a person noticed. Large and dark blue, they spoke volumes about her mood without her saying a word.

She swung a look back at Hillary. "Are you going to make that recipe for pigeon pie?"

The cook shook her head adamantly, topknot swaying. "It's barbaric."

Gwen tipped her head slightly toward him. "Would you try it?"

Instead of a challenge, he heard genuine interest. "I'd try it." He let his gaze drift to her lips. Flashes of this softer, gentler side of her were even more disturbing than the flaring spirit he'd seen earlier. "I like to taste new things."

A palm already against the door, she swiveled slowly to look back over her shoulder at him. "Do you?"

"Definitely." For a long second her eyes held his, and all the sharp words previously exchanged melted beneath one heated look. Jack swore to himself. If he wasn't careful, she could get under his skin.

Gwen breezed past the living room, saw that Trish and Wesley were alone, then hurried to her bedroom. Her nerves were still jumping. She'd seen a hint of a gentler side of him when she'd offered the apology. If he had just stuck with playing the mean cop, she wouldn't have felt unsettled by him. When they'd first met, her impression of him hadn't been good. She sensed a strong-willed and pushy nature from too many years of playing the tough guy. Now she felt differently. There was something about him. His eyes? she wondered. They could look cold as ice, but then he would smile and they'd warm, reminding her of a pale summer sky.

Such fanciful thinking, she thought. Maybe it was because she'd cut herself off too long from male companionship. By choice, she'd spent months without a man in her life. She'd needed time as a leveler after Justin.

Not wanting to have to hear a lecture about always being late, she hurried to change for dinner. Opening the shower door, she thought, with an almost painful honesty, of how shy she had become of relationships. She wasn't sure she'd ever want to take a chance on anyone again, much less someone like the sergeant, with whom she had so little in common.

At six-thirty, she entered the dining room and was struck by the sight of Trish looking comatose, a fist propped beneath her chin. Droning on incessantly was her intended's pedantic voice. Wesley gave Gwen a quick nod of greeting, as if she'd never been out of the country, and plodded on about rational economic expectations. Gwen had a few expectations herself, like a little laughter at the dinner table.

"Not everyone learns from their mistakes," her father countered in response to something Wesley had said.

Sensing the remark was aimed at herself, Gwen kept her eyes riveted on her wineglass to avoid her father's meaningful glare.

"Gwen, if Ardelle doesn't arrive soon, you'll need to play hostess at a luncheon for your sister next Saturday."

Gwen stalled, taking a sip of wine. "I won't be able to." She sent Trish an apologetic look. "I'm sorry, but—"

With a quick shake of her head, Trish reached across the table and squeezed her hand. "I know you have something planned for that day. I told—"

"What do you have planned that could be more important than your sister's wedding?" Her father's voice deepened with a familiar disapproval.

Gwen dodged his question, not wanting her first dinner with them in months to be tense. "Ardelle will be here in time," she said weakly, her voice trailing off as she noticed Jack suddenly standing in the doorway. Act I, Scene I, she mused. "Darling," Gwen gushed brightly, rushing from her chair to Jack. She placed a hand on Jack's shoulder and leaned closer, breezing a kiss past his cheek.

As she drew back, her "darling" had other ideas. His arm firm around her waist, he yo-yoed her back and glued her to his hip, flattening her breast against his chest.

"Is this the bridegroom to be, sweetheart?" he asked, stepping forward with her and offering his hand to Wesley.

He moonlighted on the stage, Gwen decided.

"We're going to have another wedding soon." Trish bubbled appropriately as Gwen led Jack to the table. "Isn't that wonderful, Wesley?"

Gwen flashed a smile while Jack remained straight-faced.

"This is Jack Mallory," her father announced to Wesley, eyeing Jack with a fatherly look of warning to keep his hands off his daughter.

Jack seemed unfazed; Gwen wondered if he was a kindred soul. Despite a disciplined job, was he as much a maverick as she was? Perhaps he didn't like taking orders, just giving them.

Through dinner her father skillfully guided Wesley away from asking too many questions about their whirlwind courtship. Since she hadn't yet received all her cue cards, Gwen was grateful. She knew practically zilch about her "beloved."

Staring at the pale rose liquid in her wineglass, she endured Wesley's monologue about the banking system for several minutes. Stifling a yawn, she cut in, "Tomorrow, you'll have to join us for dinner again, Wesley. I'm trying to talk Hillary into making a recipe I brought home with me for Moroccan pigeon pie."

Wesley paled.

Gwen felt a thread of genuine amusement taking over. "Relax. Hillary had the same reaction. We decided on a compromise—two pies. One with pigeon, the other with chicken."

Trish prodded with a nod of her head. "You didn't—you didn't really eat p-pigeons?"

"Rode a camel, too," Gwen replied, delighting in teasing her sister and the stuffy man sitting near her. "All over Morocco."

"Oh, how could you?" Trish murmured.

"They stink," Wesley piped in.

Poor Trish, Gwen mused. Wesley was as narrow-minded and unyielding as their poker-faced brother-in-law. Gloom immediately descended on a room when Ralston entered it. Though Gwen had made peace with her father and enjoyed Trish's company, on every occasion, she inevitably would ruffle the feathers of certain blue-blooded relatives like her Aunt Ursula, her older sister Ardelle or the dreary Ralston. As Wesley continued to frown, she felt an impish urge to annoy him even more. "Now how would you know how a camel smells if you've never ridden one?"

"They must smell," he countered with his usual obnoxious certainty.

"No worse than some two-legged animals," Gwen assured him.

Trish gaped, Wesley blustered to a beet red, and her father shook his head slowly in amused exasperation. But it was the sound of a soft, throaty chuckle that grabbed her attention. One look at the slip of a crooked smile on Jack's face and she couldn't help wondering if she might have found an ally.

\* \* \*

Dinner wasn't what Jack expected. Instead of rich foods, foreign to his taste buds, they ate a favorite of Gwen's, lamb chops and mint jelly.

In parting, the future bridegroom offered a limp-wrist handshake and a stuffy goodbye to Jack. Instantly he understood why Gwen was less than enamored with Wesley.

As Bowman and Trish met Earl outside the door, Earl grimaced behind their backs when he learned his evening would be chauffeuring them to a theater where some arty foreign film with subtitles was playing. The other driver, Lyndon, wasn't making out much better. Ashcroft finished his brandy, called Lyndon on the house phone, and instructed him to bring a car around. He had an evening business meeting.

Ashcroft wasn't making their job of protecting him easy. An influential man, he expected people to do things his way. "You're staying home?" His question to Gwen was almost a command.

She appeared ready to argue then gave a shrug of resignation. Jack discerned the retreat took a great deal from her. She glanced back at him.

"Do you play checkers?" she asked with a hint of impatience.

He considered a half dozen other things he'd rather do, but nodded agreeably. Protective-custody assignments never had appealed to him. He didn't like being closeted with one person constantly, having no time alone. But a game of checkers would beat staring at a television screen. On other similar assignments, he'd done that more times than he'd wanted to.

Meeting her intelligent blue eyes, he thought she might just play a shrewd game.

"I'll be home early," Ashcroft said from the archway. He didn't seem interested in a response, and neither of them offered one.

Leaning against the stone hearth, Jack kept his eyes on Gwen. She crouched before a cabinet and withdrew a box of checkers. When the front door slammed, her shoulders dropped noticeably. He got the odd impression that she seemed more a stranger in the house than himself.

Placing the checkerboard on the table, her hands stilled, and eyes that seemed too perceptive suddenly met his. "Would you help me?"

He'd pushed away from the hearth to join her, but, rocked by her question, hesitated in mid-stride. "Help? With what?" he asked, feeling tension prickle at the back of his neck. He could tell by her tone, her eyes, she wasn't talking about checkers.

She drifted to the stereo in a corner of the room and flicked on music.

It was a light classical piece that Jack couldn't name. "Help with what?" he repeated.

She didn't join him at the table. "I need ideas. I seem to have run dry," she said, sounding amazed it could have happened. "Don't you have any ideas for getting Trish to listen to me? Despite what everyone else thinks, Fred is the one for her."

"I'm not trained at meddling."

Her head snapped up. "It's not meddling." She looked genuinely affronted. "My sister will be miserable with Wesley. I have to find a way to prevent their marriage."

"And so you'll use this guy Fred to do it."

"I don't *use* people," she said in a voice suddenly edged with irritation, her eyes darkening as a flush of anger swept over her face. *"Never."*

"Easy," he soothed, aware he'd pricked a raw spot.

"You don't understand," she said quietly again. "Trish loves Fred. That's why I have to stop her marriage to Wesley." Gwen knew she was rambling, but she couldn't stop herself. He was too quiet for her; it made her wonder what he was thinking. "Now do you understand?"

"Not really. What's Fred's problem? Why doesn't he fit the Ashcroft family plan? Questionable beginnings?"

"*I* certainly don't believe in questionable beginnings," she said and stared down at her own hand as if it were unfamiliar. "But come to think of it, our engagement might be viewed as one. I seem to be missing the symbolic engagement ring."

"Talk to Daddy."

She dropped her hand to her side and looked at him thoughtfully. "Are you getting even with me for the way I acted earlier?"

Jack saw genuine concern in her face. "Do you think I should?"

Her eyes stirred uneasily as if her next words were too painful. "I was incorrigible."

He couldn't really disagree. She had acted just as he'd expected. Uncooperative. But then he had thought it was connected to spoiled, rich beginnings. He was beginning to think differently.

She sent him a sad smile. "Your silences are very eloquent, Sergeant."

As she strolled toward the archway, he wondered if she'd changed her mind about the game.

"I'll be right back," she called out.

He watched her disappear. Despite preconceived notions that she would be difficult to deal with, he couldn't find fault with her. Outgoing, she seemed now to be sincerely interested in reaching a level of compatibility necessary for getting through difficult moments together. He'd expected someone different. Ghosts of the past, he decided, recalling Christina and her snide friends.

Hearing the quick click of heels touching the gleaming foyer floor, he looked up. Head bent, she reentered the room, carrying a tray. She gave off a contradictory image. Though her clothes were casual, a creamy white silk blouse and slacks, she looked classy—too classy to be waiting on anyone.

The moment she drew near, he caught a whiff of the same subtle scent that had lingered around him during dinner. It was a fragile scent, the fragrance of blossoms that reminded him of a spring day and a stroll past a flower garden in Lincoln Park.

She set the tray on a nearby table. "I brought coffee."

"Isn't Horton around?"

"In the kitchen. He and Hillary are having their dinner."

An intriguing woman, Jack mused. He'd assumed that she would expect the royal treatment. Because he couldn't get a handle on her, neither could he ignore her. He liked puzzles. He'd gone into police work, thinking it would be a natural occupation for him. He liked piecing together the unknowns, searching for the missing parts to solve crimes. He wondered what it was that made this woman so unlike the others in her family.

"Did you like Wesley?" she asked, staring down at the board as he moved a checker.

Jack rocked a hand in a so-so gesture. "Why don't *you* like him? What's wrong with him?" he prodded, both out of personal curiosity and concern for a possible leak. Though Farrow was behind the threats, the captain had considered the possibility that Farrow might use someone acquainted with the Ashcrofts to do the dirty work. There were a lot of ways to persuade people to help. "His credentials are good enough, aren't they?"

"They're superb. But he's after Trish's money."

Jack registered her comment and wondered if Bowman's money problems would make him vulnerable to Farrow.

"Socially he's considered a great catch," she admitted. "He's from a banking family. His great-great-whatever-grandfather founded their first one."

Jack sent her a puzzled look. "If his family's in banking, why would he be after her money?"

"To have more of it. Wesley has a rivalry going on with his older brother. It's about who can make more millions at a younger age. His brother seems to have hit a financial plateau at thirty-one. Understand?''

He really didn't. "Are you saying that he'd marry her to get another million before his brother—"

"To prove that he's better than his brother. If marriage is the only way, then why not?"

"How do you know that?"

The corners of her lips curled into a smile. "The day before I left for Europe, Wesley was falling down drunk and spilled the beans—while also trying to relieve me of my clothes. It was easy enough to evade him. He was so tipsy.

"I kept circling the sofa, and he kept stumbling after me. In the process, I asked him questions, and since he was more preoccupied with my chest than my questions, he told me his plans."

Jack was amused at her cleverness. "So he told you all of this?"

"Yes, he did. And I tried to tell Trish, but she was deaf. My timing was off. She might have listened more, but Wesley was charming her, and Fred was growing insane with jealousy, and she was confused about both men's actions. So when I told her about Wesley, she ignored me."

Jack's information about Gladstone was scant, but he couldn't imagine Fred having any more of the right credentials to marry an Ashcroft than he did himself. "How can you be sure this old boyfriend is right for her?"

"Oh, Fred's right for her. There's no doubt about that."

"He's not after her money?"

"Could be," she admitted between sips of coffee, "but that doesn't matter."

He stared at her hand on the cup. It was slender like her, her fingers long and delicate-looking. "Why doesn't it matter if Fred's after her money?"

"I'm pretty sure he's not, but even if he is, it's okay. Because he loves her. He's *wild* about my sister. It's all right to marry for money if you love that person, too."

"And he needs money?"

"I wouldn't know. I doubt it. The Gladstones own several dairy farms in Wisconsin. Fred is a fifth-generation owner. But my aunt still visualizes Trish milking cows."

Jack looked down as she finally moved another checker. "So what happened between Fred and your sister? Why'd they split up?"

"They had a lovers' spat. And stupidly, he attended a party with someone else. Trish is stubborn. She won't forgive him."

Jack scanned the checkerboard. As she'd chatted, she'd been gathering momentum against him.

"So," she said, as he began to make his move, "tell me about yourself. We really do need to know more about each other."

Jack didn't think so. He shared his time but rarely his feelings with others. Other than Earl and his wife, he kept to himself. He had no problems with solitude. Early in life, he had learned to be satisfied with only his own company.

"Have you been a policeman long?"

"Eleven years."

"So you're experienced enough for this job."

"I'm experienced enough for most things." Jack jumped one of her checkers as he said it, making her wince.

She recovered quickly. "Do you have family nearby?"

"I don't have anyone," he said. He scooped up a red checker. "My mother died when I was young."

Running a finger along the delicate handle of her coffee cup, she stared down at the board. "And your father?"

He watched her face. Soot-black lashes hooded her eyes. He wondered if the conversation was to divert his attention from the game. "I have no idea."

As if someone had jabbed her in the middle of the back, she suddenly sat up straighter. She pretended to be studying the board, but she kept sliding her checker one way, then another, with a hesitation that seemed unnatural.

"I didn't say that to make you uncomfortable."

She raised eyes filled with compassion. "That was my line."

"You'll have to think of another."

She rolled with the blunt punch he'd thrown, as if experienced at absorbing sharp responses. She spoke as if searching the wall behind him for words. "Well, let's see. How about—"

For some reason, he felt rotten.

She stared at him with eyes that still carried an apology. "It's an interesting way to start out. How fortunate for you."

As she looked at him over the rim of her coffee cup, he was suddenly aware that she wasn't like any woman he'd ever met. Whatever he'd thought before about the assignment, he knew one thing now. It wasn't going to be a dull one. In only a few minutes, he had learned something vital about her. While she uttered some statements for shock value, she was hiding a delicate, sensitive soul. She also played one hell of a game of checkers, he mused, as he looked down at his side of the board.

"King me," she said, her eyes suddenly sparkling at him.

She'd get the better of him in a lot of ways if he wasn't careful, he decided.

## Chapter Three

Morning sunlight highlighted sun-bleached strands in his hair. Gwen stood by her bedroom window, watching him. Standing on the flagstone walkway under a giant willow, he stared at the woods that backed the house. He seemed to be doing nothing, but Gwen had already noted that he never wasted a moment. Even when his eyes appeared expressionless, he was observing people, scanning his surroundings. She assumed the ability to remain so still, to be so quiet, made him a good cop—alert to the slightest movement, the faintest sound.

She, on the other hand, needed action, noise, movement. She'd always hated the degree of nervous energy within her, envied those people who could so calmly just sit back to read a book and relax. Relaxing to her came in a different way, and it meant not standing still. He was just the opposite, a quiet man of few words who appeared perfectly content alone.

Jack considered the day ahead. Whatever she wanted to do, wherever she wanted to go, he'd be with her. The surprising coziness he felt at constantly being with someone was proving to be the most difficult part of his duty. Difficult, if he got too used to it.

As Gwen strolled toward him from the back of the house, for the first time in five years he felt a distinct thrill at just watching one particular woman walk.

She looked trim, almost fragile, in black tights and bright blue leg warmers. A scooped top hid nothing of her soft curves. "I hope you've had breakfast."

As she slipped on an oversize pale blue shirt that covered all her alluring curves, he tossed his cigarette to the ground. "Where are we going?"

"Not far. A fifteen-minute drive." She handed him a bright paisley shoulder bag to hold while she bent to fish around in it. Finally she yanked out a long tortoiseshell barrette. "Well, have you eaten breakfast?"

Jack dangled the bag from his fingers. "Hours ago."

"Ever sleep, Sergeant?" she teased, clipping back her hair.

"Enough of this," he said distractedly, wondering if her hair felt as soft as it looked. He shoved the bag back at her. "I'll get the car," he said in a tone more clipped than he'd intended, betraying his sudden impulse to put distance between them.

As she'd promised, the drive was short—but unnaturally silent. That bothered him. He was becoming used to her talking to him.

"Turn here," she finally said, as he neared the town square. "See the big building?"

"The movie theater?"

"It used to be one. Turn into the parking lot near it," she instructed, pointing at a sign for Camelot Dance Studios.

He'd expected her to go to a health club, some place where she'd be pampered afterward. "Do you have a class?"

"Several."

As she grabbed the bright paisley-colored bag from the floor of the car, Jack considered the morning ahead of him. Eyeing women in leotards wouldn't be such a bad way to pass the time.

He followed her into the studio and paused in the doorway, not forgetting for a second the real reason he was with her. Scanning the front office, he noted that it had three windows close to the ceiling—inaccessible windows, too high for an intruder. And the only other doorway, besides the one he was standing in, was a fire exit. He would check it in a moment.

"Excuse me," a small voice said behind him.

Jack stepped aside and looked down. An urchin, probably no older than eight, gave him a missing-tooth grin.

Her eyes rounded like saucers as the girl stared past him to Gwen. "Miss Ashcroft." Excitement rose in her voice. "You're back."

Jack was still entranced by the first girl's delight when three more, of various sizes, skittered past him. All of them were dressed in leotards. So much for a morning of ogling, he thought, amused.

"I had to come back," he heard Gwen say, as the little girls circled around her. As she dropped to a crouch to be at their eye level, Jack realized that he had too many misconceptions about her. She was obviously the owner of the dance studio and just as obviously well-liked by her students.

"The big recital is on Saturday, isn't it?" she asked, smiling.

Little heads nodded in unison.

She touched the top of a braided one. "How are your pirouettes?"

The girl's face turned glum.

"We'll work on them together," Gwen assured her, reviving the girl's sunshine smile.

"Gwen, you have a load of messages." The woman behind the desk was slim, probably in her late twenties. Good-looking with shiny brown hair, her few words showed a trace of a Southwestern accent. She turned watery brown eyes up at Jack, then discreetly sent Gwen a speculative look.

Gwen's shoulders straightened noticeably as she was forced to utter the lie again. Glancing at Jack, she closed the space between them, hooked an arm in his, and whipped up a convincing brightness. "Carrie, I have wonderful news. I got engaged."

The woman looked astonished. "Engaged?" Jack sensed that behind her bewilderment lay some knowledge about her employer's personal life that made the lie less believable. What is going on? her eyes seemed to say, even as she jumped from the chair to congratulate them.

Gwen went through the motions. She smiled, she hugged, she pretended admirably.

But Jack caught the sadness briefly clouding her eyes. She was a breath away from denying everything. As Carrie resettled behind the desk, he moved quickly and slipped an arm around Gwen's waist. "You did great," he said softly against her ear.

She forced a smile. "Why does the idea of being a great liar not thrill me?" She stepped forward again to scoop up the pile of papers Carrie had indicated. "Thanks, Carrie."

"You're welcome," she answered, her eyes smiling at Jack over the top of a tissue jammed against her nose.

Gwen paused, tilting her head questioningly. "Do you have a cold again?"

Laughing, Carrie raised a hand as if warding off evil. "No cold. Allergies," she said lightly. "I couldn't handle another bout with your famous remedy. She spent an entire night pumping it into me," she told Jack.

They shared a quick, comfortable moment of amusement before Gwen turned back to Jack. "I can give you a cup of coffee in my office."

"Sounds good."

She said a few more words to the girls gathered nearby, then led the way down a long hallway of closed doors.

Behind each door they passed, there was the hint of music. "What's the cold remedy?" Jack asked out of curiosity.

"Lemon, whisky, tea, and a touch of garlic." She sniffed demonstrably. "A winner for clearing the sinuses."

He set his stride to match hers. "You sure are a concerned employer—nursing runny-nosed receptionists through the night."

Gwen slanted a look at him. "Carrie is my best friend."

And that made the lie more difficult, he realized.

"We trust each other." She slowed her pace as she talked. "I could never have left the studio to travel without knowing she was here. And now look at how I return that trust."

Again he caught the flicker of despair. "She won't hold the lie against you."

"I hope not. She and Gloria—" She paused at an open door and indicated the fair-haired woman in front of a class. "The three of us have been friends since college. Friends deserve the truth," she said, leading the way to a door with her name on it.

Jack lingered in the doorway. Her office with its gleaming wood floor, mirrored wall and ballet bar wasn't like any office he'd ever seen before. "Do you dance?"

She raised her eyes from papers on a small Queen Anne desk. "Instruct. I was never dedicated enough to be a prima ballerina. And I kept hearing too much rhythm in my head. But I've studied all different kinds of dance. I had the funds to open the studio, so I did."

"You hardly have to work."

She rounded the desk to reach her chair. "What would I do, Sergeant? I'm not the charity fund-raiser type or the perfect hostess of a mansion." She gave him an amused grin. "You had unfavorable thoughts about us, didn't you? Idle rich. Spoiled brats." At his silence, she chided. "I think you're a bit of a snob, too, Sergeant."

That was the last description he'd ever expected to receive. Hard-nosed, unfeeling, cold and a few other choice words had been hurled at him during his career on the force, but never that one. He had to admit that she showed genuine warmth for her family, a committed interest in her students, and deep concern for a friend. Okay, he thought, she can't be pigeon-holed, but she still wasn't the All-American girl next door, either.

"You don't really know me," she said, feeling a need to remind him.

Jack passed her desk on his way to the windows. "No, I don't, but then I don't know too many people who just traipse off to Europe."

"Oh, I see. You assume that I went there to do nothing but visit some decadent rich friends," she said bluntly meaning to put him in his place. He swung around and she could barely hold on to her quiet tone. "Well, I was visiting a few friends in Europe, but I wasn't vacationing. I went there to attend a seminar about choreography being given by Madame Felicia. She was a prima ballerina before a car accident put her in a wheelchair. Today she runs a dance studio in France for only the most promising ballerinas."

Jack leaned against the wall by the windows, noting that even as she talked she nervously riffled through her messages. "What were you doing in Morocco?"

"I've been dying to learn a few secrets of legitimate belly dancers."

"And did you?" he asked, eyeing the exit door to outside and wondering if it was easily accessible from the street.

"The steps only, not the technique."

Jack checked the locked door, relieved to find a dead bolt.

"Rolling one's belly is not as simple as it sounds."

He chuckled and watched her scan her messages again. Reaching for the telephone, she looked all business. "I'll be here several hours," she said as she dialed. "If you want to leave—"

"I'll stay." He wandered around the room checking the rest of the windows and the closet, then wound up back at the door.

Cradling the receiver between her jaw and shoulder, she smiled. "Is my fortress secure?"

"Adequate. I'll check out the building and be back."

"You'll stir a lot of excitement."

A hand on the doorknob, he turned to her with a questioning look.

"I only have a few male students." The tease was back in her eyes. "And none of them look like you."

Two hours later, Gwen had finished making her phone calls, visiting classes and checking the costumes for the recitals. As she stepped back into her office, she flicked on the tape recorder at the edge of a shelf. It had been a long time since she'd worked out. She'd gone to Europe for one other reason—to forget Justin Bennett. She'd succeeded in pushing aside hurt and anger, but she wondered if she would ever learn to fully trust any man again.

Music floated into the room, the lilting tones of "Scheherezade." She positioned herself by the bar and moved through a slow arabesque. She dreamed of the desert, of exotic scents, of tents, and a mysterious sheikh. It was music to suit her mood. But before she saw Jack again, she thought, she'd have to switch to a peppier beat, some tune that wasn't so sultry, so sensual.

She was warming to him. When she'd talked about Carrie and the trust between them, she'd felt his understanding. She hadn't expected such gentle responses from him. She hadn't thought he would be an easy man to get to know.

Determinedly she concentrated again on her dancing, until a heated tiredness clung to her muscles. She thought about the need she felt to nurture the children's pleasure. Few in her family would ever understand. They were too content with the silver spoon. She wanted to succeed on her own, do something besides propagate the family's good name.

Twirling rhythmically, she ignored aching muscles, and responded to the rushed tempo of a new song— the pounding beat of a boogie. Arms up, out, another twirl, a leg kick. She swallowed against the dryness in her throat, as the exhilaration continued to pump through her. On another quick twirl, she faced the mirror and came to an abrupt stop, her leg stretched out to the side, her arms up in a triumphant gesture.

And then she saw him.

In the shadows of the darkening room, he stood watching her. And though his eyes appeared like slits, she could feel their intensity.

Gwen raised a hand to brush hair from her face. A melody seemed to fill her, humming to near explosion. She couldn't ignore the pressure in her chest, the shortness of breath that had little to do with exertion and more to do with the pale eyes staring at her in the silence.

She watched him drag his gaze away from the cloth straining against her breasts to peer into her eyes. "I'll be ready soon," she said between breaths, suddenly unsteady.

"I'll wait outside."

She heard him curse softly before closing the door behind him. How with one look did he challenge every female instinct within her? Why did she let him? Annoyed suddenly, she shrugged back into her oversize shirt. It was nonsense, she assured herself, and snatching at her purse, she strolled toward the door.

The moment she stepped outside, he flung open the car door. "Do you need to go anywhere else?"

She noticed the grim set of his mouth and shook her head, grateful that he was willing to treat the previous moment as if it had never happened.

"Then there's nothing else?"

"No, nothing," she assured him, her pulse still beating too fast.

Jack kept his eyes on the traffic, wishing he could get out of his head the image of her dancing. He could still see her, the soft misty sheen clinging to her arms and the sweat-soaked top plastered to her, hugging her breasts like a second skin and outlining her nipples. She hadn't looked like the master-of-the-manor's daughter. Winded, her face glowing, she'd made him forget who she was.

Pulling up in front of the house, he was almost glad to see it. It stood large and imposing, a reminder of what he couldn't afford to forget. *She* belonged here; *he* didn't.

Braking, Jack watched Earl lift himself from his position against the family limo. Parked behind it was a gray one.

"We've got a problem," he said approaching Jack's car. He shot back a look at the gray limo as if it were the cause of his trouble. "The other sister is here. Ardelle Van Hammon."

In the passenger seat, Gwen lunged forward to retrieve her purse from the floor. As she straightened, Jack saw her frown. Without a word, she left the car and hurried into the house.

"She wasn't supposed to come home until next week," Earl told Jack. "And damn if the husband isn't with her."

Jack's gaze followed Gwen until the front door closed behind her. Judging from her reaction, he doubted the oldest Ashcroft daughter was as sweet and complacent as Trish or as spirited and intriguing as Gwen.

Spirited? Intriguing? Where the hell had that come from? When had he begun to think of her that way? he wondered.

"Jack?" Earl was trying to get his attention.

As he turned to him, Jack caught his puzzled stare and ignored it. Keep your mind on the job, he berated himself, and concentrate on the problem of protecting two more people earlier than expected. "Call Caulder. Tell him we need more help," he told Earl.

"Yeah. I think we might," Earl said suspiciously.

Good friend that he was, he said nothing else. But the words he'd left unsaid came through clearly. Be careful. She's out of your league.

Gwen paused in the foyer to firmly plaster a bright smile on her face for her older sister. Dealing with Ardelle would take all her energies. The last thing she needed was to suddenly find herself wrestling against a rush of attraction for her fake fiancé. She was determined not to let it happen again.

For the next five minutes, she forced herself to ooh and aah over Ardelle's latest buys as her sister made a ceremony out of opening the various bags and boxes from Saks and I. Magnin and displaying each of her new purchases.

Holding up a lilac silk pantsuit, Ardelle riveted a critical gaze on Gwen, then touched a strand of her hair. "You do plan to have your hair styled for the wedding, don't you?"

Gwen saved her sister from putting her foot in her mouth. "I will, for the wedding," she promised, willing to make that concession for Trish's sake.

Ardelle stood before them—her regal posture, her impeccably coiffured blond hair, and her black Halston with strands of gold wound around her neck— and played queen. As the oldest sister, she seemed to accept that as her rightful position. Gwen could recall being closer as children, but after their mother's death, her sister had become more self-absorbed and they'd grown apart. Today she had her charities, her committees, her position as Ralston's wife, and little in common with Gwen.

"I remember my own wedding to Ralston." Ardelle fingered the silk of her latest buy. "I was just useless. Absolutely useless for months before it. Aren't you excited?"

Trish spoke her line on cue but a touch too gaily to be convincing. "Oh, I am."

"Where will you go for your honeymoon, Trish? Saint Moritz?" Ardelle repacked her bags slowly. "I talked to Bunny Hentford two days ago. She said that Monaco is lovely this time of year."

"I haven't been to Switzerland in ages," Trish returned.

"If you don't honeymoon there, then go with me after Christmas."

"That would be nice."

"After your divorce, Trish," Gwen quipped.

"Oh, you are going to be sour, aren't you?" Ardelle scolded in a between-the-teeth deliverance.

"No, I'm not." Gwen widened her lips into a smile that threatened to crack her face.

Casting Gwen a dubious look, Ardelle finally settled on the sofa beside Trish.

"Have you met Gwen's fiancé yet?" Trish piped in, seeming to relish being the one to drop the bomb.

Ardelle froze, gaping, the coffee cup hanging between two fingers in midair. "F-fiancé?"

Innocence personified, Gwen shrugged a shoulder, wondering how much more deception would follow.

"Whooo?" her sister asked, imitating an owl.

The lie sticking in her throat, Gwen clung as close to the truth as she could. "A man I met recently." As Ardelle leaned forward and ceremoniously set her cup and saucer back on the table, Gwen slanted a deadly look at Trish. She looked ready to explode with laughter.

"And what does *this one* do to earn a living?"

Gwen couldn't blame her older sister for being wary. Some previous choices had hardly ranked among the acceptable type. "He, uh, was in oil," she said, remembering her father's words about Jack's Oklahoma oil-rigging background. "But he's in securities now," she answered brightly.

Ardelle's eyes no longer resembled marbles. "I wonder if Ralston knows him."

Gwen chose the easiest path. "Perhaps."

Ardelle fiddled with the silver sugar prongs. "Well, does he know any of our friends—someone who could give him a recommendation?"

"He's not applying for a job," Gwen reminded her.

Her sister's nose raised to a regal tilt. "He's being considered to join our family."

"No consideration. If I want to marry him, I will."

"Family approval is important, many things have to be considered." Ardelle sipped her coffee. "I hope he's more suitable than Fred Gladstone was."

Gwen saw sadness cloud Trish's eyes. "There was nothing wrong with Fred. And Jack is—"

"Jack? That's his first name?"

"Mallory. Jack Mallory."

"What kind of name is that? Irish?"

Gwen heaved a sigh, realizing how much she wanted to snap at her sister for forcing more pretense on her. "Ardelle, I don't know, and I don't care. I'm hot for the man," she flared instead.

Choking on her coffee, Ardelle grabbed a napkin and quickly dabbed at a drop on her chin. "I refuse to respond to such a remark."

The conversation moved on from a discussion about an incompetent manicurist to a party spoiled by bad caviar. Gwen could stand it for only a few minutes. "I'm going for a walk," she announced.

Ardelle's eyes darkened with irritation. "Gwen, you're in the bridal party. You should want to be a part of our discussion."

"Oh, I do." She'd willingly appease Ardelle to avoid hurting Trish's feelings. "But I need to change for dinner."

Behind her, she heard Ardelle mumble something sympathetic to Trish. Gwen wasn't interested in hearing it. She knew Ardelle's opinion of her manner. Every family needed its black sheep, she reasoned.

Sidestepping the butler, she rushed toward the front door. She needed fresh air before she smothered.

Jack had wandered into the kitchen and away from the cultured sounds of Gwen's older sister. He didn't think he'd like her.

At the banging of pots, he looked up. Hillary scurried from a cabinet to the stove. Saffron and cinnamon mingled together from a large kettle and permeated the air. "She talked you into making that recipe, didn't she?"

With a quick grin, Hillary stirred the contents of the pot. "She's difficult to refuse. But Miss Ardelle will have fits."

"Does that worry you?"

"Since their mama died, she's taken over the running of the household." She grinned wide and raised the spoon from the pot. "Would you like to sample the dinner?"

"If I begged, would you forget to set my plate at the table?"

The older woman chuckled. "No. You promised Miss Gwen."

Jack paused at the door. "You're heartless, Hillary." As he closed the door behind him, he saw the silhouette of a woman leaning against a giant willow. Moonlight slanted a silver glow across her red hair. Though the house was guarded, she was vulnerable outside alone. A cop's instinct made him scan the darkness of the woods while he cursed himself for assuming that Gwen was in the house, a captive audience for her older sister.

Approaching her, he saw her paleness in the moonlight, and something in her stance, her slender shoulders turned in, made him slow his stride and ease his mood. "Is that tree your personal leaning post?"

As if it were heavy, she raised her head slowly from its bowed position. "For the moment."

Jack stopped an arm's length from her. "What are you doing here?"

"Breathing." Head bent again, she pushed away from the tree to stroll toward a white wrought-iron bench.

Jack sensed the distance she wanted couldn't be found on the Ashcroft premises. "You can't be wandering around alone," he said, feeling like apologizing for doing his job.

"I'm sorry," she said in an unnaturally dull voice. "I don't mean to cause you problems." Shivering, she hugged herself though Jack felt no chill. "I'm like the square peg in the round hole around here."

As she stared at the dark woods, he yearned for her feisty spirit. Earlier, watching her dance, he'd marveled at her energy, her endurance. He could have watched her for hours then. The easy suppleness of her movements, even just her walk, had attracted him from the beginning. She was all grace—elegant, poised, agile. When she danced, moisture had clung to her skin, bathing it, but she'd looked cool; he was the one who'd felt hot.

Now, in the shadowy light, she was enveloped in a pale soft glow, her hair flowing back from her face beneath the gentle breeze. He wanted to touch the fiery strands, to feel the silky texture beneath his fingers.

"I need to get away." Her appeal stretched between them. "Somewhere."

"Where?"

"Anywhere."

## Chapter Four

Jack acted on impulse. Because she looked as if she needed a friend more than anything else, he felt safe dropping his guard with her. He took her to an all-night diner famous for chili hamburgers.

"Thank you," she said as if he'd given her some precious gift.

"For a beer?" He noticed that she hadn't even lifted her mug.

"For a few quiet moments."

He stretched his legs beneath the table, careful not to touch her. "What's the problem? Is it your sister's arrival?"

Gwen shook her head. "No, Ardelle and I have always opposed each other. I'm used to squabbles with her. But I'm so worried for Trish. She's so young, and she's going to make a terrible mistake. I don't know why she won't admit that she's in love with Fred," she said with open frustration.

"Could be that you're wrong."

"I'm not," Gwen said firmly. "But for some reason Fred buckled. He shouldn't have let her slip away. He's too intimidated by Ralston. Every time Fred came here, Ralston had Wesley with him. I suppose Fred stupidly believed that Trish found Wesley attractive. But from what my sister's told me, she and Fred have never really talked out their problem." She heaved a sigh of exasperation. "It's all one big misunderstanding now. Why don't people talk more?" she asked, incredulously.

Jack considered the simplicity of her question. "Why would I think that you'd be a firm believer in that?"

"Because I'm a blabbermouth," she said without hesitation. With effort, she tried to smile.

"What's really wrong?"

She visibly folded. "The lies. I hate the lies to Ardelle, to Carrie."

He leaned back in the booth, because suddenly with only the table separating them, it was too easy to touch her hand. "They're necessary," Jack reminded her.

"Necessary lies? My family has been split so many years because of what were considered *necessary lies*. But I'll always wonder if they were really necessary."

He prodded, not out of curiosity, but out of a need to offer what she seemed to need most at the moment—someone to listen to her. "Why don't you think they were?"

"Because they did too much harm. I wasn't home for years because of them," she said softly, seeming to not want to admit it. "When my father met my mother, she was a dancer in an off-Broadway musical."

Jack looked up from his beer, confused by the information. Professional dancers didn't usually come from wealthy beginnings. "She wasn't born of the manor?"

"No." She shook her head. "Definitely not aristocratic stock." As she frowned again, he wanted to lean forward and touch the line marring her brow. "I missed her terribly when she died. Months before that, she indicated that she wanted to return to dancing. My father wouldn't let her go." She said it almost as if talking to herself.

The words poured from her easily, perhaps because he was still a stranger. She couldn't explain it any other way. She told him things she had never shared with anyone else. "When she died a short time later, I thought that he was wrong. I thought that she'd shriveled up because she'd been denied that chance, and I held it against my father for years. I'd believed that he'd used us, my sisters and myself, to keep her from doing it, to make her feel guilty about leaving us for even a short amount of time. I couldn't hold back the bitterness. Missing her terribly, I said some hurtful things to him." Sadness clung to her voice. "When I was old enough, I took off."

He watched a ring of cigarette smoke hang in the air. He'd joined the police force for a sense of belonging. Never having had a family himself, he couldn't imagine anyone willingly walking away from one.

"One day I was home for the holidays, and the truth came out. My mother had only told us she wanted to return to dancing so she could leave and spare us from seeing her grow weaker with sickness. My father claimed that she believed it was a necessary lie."

Jack strained to hear her words over the cacophony of shrill electric guitars from a jukebox in the corner. He deciphered bitterness and hurt, but it was the shame she felt, so evident in the words wrenched from her, that made him want to make her stop, tell her not to reopen old wounds.

"My father broke down and told me that he'd loved her too much to let her go. He'd wanted every second he could have with her."

"Why didn't he tell you that before?"

Her hands cupped tightly around the beer mug; she showed him the semblance of a smile. "I'm not surprised you said that. It's logical. I asked him that too, remembering all the dreadful things that I'd said to him. He said that we'd both been hurting too much to think clearly. But I felt so much pain and sadness the day he told me the truth, because I'd let anger and then pride keep us apart for so long. For years I had pushed him away." She turned anguished eyes up at Jack. "Maybe if I hadn't, if I had stayed, he would have said something sooner. But for years I held bitterness toward him inside me. I did some foolish things."

"How old were you when she died?"

She sent him a puzzled look. "Ten."

"Kids do things to get even."

Venting some of her own pain had eased her. Jack had made her feel less alone. Kind, he was kind, she realized in that instant. "It's too bad it took me so long to grow up."

He started to reach forward to touch her hand but stopped himself. While he could fight an attraction—maybe—he wondered how he would ever distance himself from a longing to comfort her.

She was silent, disturbingly so as Jack drove her home. When he opened the car door for her, she hesitated as if lost in her own world of disquieting thoughts.

Dulled eyes turned up to him. "I owe my family something. Trish is still so young. She sees the world through rose-colored glasses, and Ardelle sees only her own reflection. I need to remind them and myself to look out for each other. They need to remember that we're a family. But how can we be a real family if we lie to each other?"

It wasn't a question he could answer.

"Jack, you won't let anything happen to my father, will you?"

Her plea came out in a whisper. As a cop, he tried to keep from being touched emotionally, but too many times someone had looked at him for answers as if his badge gave him some extra power. All he'd ever been able to do then was offer tokens of reassuring words. "No, I won't," he answered, realizing that for her sake, for the guilt she still seemed burdened by, for the love she wanted her family to accept, he didn't want to fail.

As they stepped from the car, he kept his distance; he felt closer to her, perhaps too close. They shared a common thread. Neither of them had known a happy childhood.

"Thank you," she said suddenly.

With a sidelong glance, he watched the evening breeze toss her hair, its dark red color lost beneath the night's shadows. From the house, he could hear faint sounds of Beethoven floating on the air.

She looked in need of a hug. It was his only thought. He caught her arm before she could turn away, and he drew her to him. As she sagged against him, he felt her draw a quick calming breath. And he felt her softness.

Excitement he hadn't expected assailed him.

When she stared up at him, he told himself it would be crazy to let feelings for this woman interfere with his job. But then he didn't feel too sensible at the moment. He also didn't feel like a man with a great deal of control. For the past few days, he'd felt an urge to touch her. What he hadn't expected was a closeness of a different kind. Like an invisible wire, it stretched between them, joining them and growing shorter every day.

Not understanding anything about his feelings at the moment, he chose the safest course of action. He released her and started to turn toward the house, but halted at the sound of something behind him. Because he'd been engrossed in her, he didn't know if it was a small animal that had wandered too close to the house or if it was a real menace. He listened again and heard the rustling of leaves from a nearby bush. In one swift move he swung around, grabbed her arm and yanked her tight against his side.

"Is there someone—" Shaken, her words trailed off like a whisper.

Squinting to see what wasn't visible, Jack gently banged his hip against hers to direct her. "Go in the house," he whispered. When she didn't move, rougher than he'd intended, he placed a hand at the small of her back and propelled her the few feet to the overhang of the house. "Stay here, then," he demanded softly.

Stay! Her heart hammering, Gwen doubted she could move. As he pressed his back to the house and inched his way toward the bushes, she craned her neck, but she couldn't see or hear anything. When he disappeared from view, fear pricked at her. She was safe, but he wasn't. Suddenly it seemed impossible to just stand still and wait.

Eyes riveted to the shrubbery, she copied Jack's movements until she reached the bushes bordering the cement walkway toward the pool. As she inched forward, she held her breath to listen. Voices muffled by the wind drifted to her. Her fingers tight on her purse straps, she gave no more thought to what she was doing and rushed forward, ready to wield the only weapon she had.

His back to her, Jack had pinned someone against the trunk of a tree. As Gwen came within steps of them, she didn't need to see the man's face to know his name.

"Let me go," a familiar male voice insisted with youthful bravado.

Gwen rushed forward.

A pale Fred swung his head to look at her wide-eyed over Jack's shoulder. "Gwen, thank God. Help me please. Tell this guy—"

"What are you doing here?" she asked, though she already knew the answer to her question. Fred had chanced the security guard and the Dobermans to see Trish.

"All I want to do is see Trish alone."

As Jack hissed with annoyance and released his grip on Fred's collar, Gwen took control of the moment. "Fred, you could have been hurt. Father has a security guard now."

"To stop me," he said in a tone that edged paranoia. "But I don't care." His melodramatic reply nearly made her smile. At twenty-one, he looked years younger when angry, like a boy annoyed that he hadn't been chosen to be the star pitcher on a baseball team. Lean, almost gaunt, he hunched his slim shoulders before letting loose his frustration. Her heart went out to him. "They let me in yesterday, but she wouldn't talk to me, and every time I came to the gate today, someone stopped me," he said hotly.

"Then why don't you get the message?" Jack cut in. "She doesn't want to see you."

Fred's back went rigid. "Who is this guy?" he demanded, gesturing with a thumb in Jack's direction.

Lies and more lies, Gwen thought dismally. "My fiancé," she said, looking over her shoulder, distracted by the sound of running footsteps.

Breathing hard, Earl's broad shoulders heaved as he stopped before them. "When the dogs started barking at the front gate, I thought there might be trouble."

Gwen shook her head. "Nothing serious." She didn't miss the meaningful look exchanged between Jack and Earl.

"So this is the fella causing all the racket," Earl said, looking at Fred disdainfully. "You should go," he said with as much authority as a chauffeur could have.

"I'm not going," Fred insisted.

"Fred, please go," she appealed, aware that without identifying themselves neither Jack nor Earl could demand he leave. "You won't see her tonight."

"Gwen—I—I can't let her marry him. I can't," he said adamantly.

"I'll tell her you were here." She placed a none-too-gentle hand on his arm and urged him to move away, but he'd planted his feet firmly.

"Will you help me?"

Gwen squeezed his arm. "I'll try." As he still hesitated, she offered more assurance. "I promise."

"And you'll call me and let me know if—"

"I'll call," she cut in. "Now, please go, before you get into real trouble."

Earl stepped closer. "Come on, kid. You don't need more trouble." At his reluctance, Earl tugged gently on his arm. "Tell me. How did you get in?"

Reluctantly Fred moved with him toward the gate. "I climbed the willow outside the security fence and crawled along the top of a wall until I reached the pool house, then I jumped onto the roof and into the yard."

Gwen heard Jack release a soft expletive over Fred's easy entry, but she was thinking of something other than his security problem. She felt annoyance with her family and Trish mingling in with irritation over the whole situation—the transformation of the manor into a fortress. "Was it necessary to treat him like that?" Though she saw temper flash in Jack's eyes, she was too irritated to be cautious. "You had no right—"

"Wake up! This isn't some game for thrills. This is real life. And your father, or any of you, could be in real danger."

"So you've said before. What kind of threats did he receive?" she demanded to know. "Phone calls don't cause this kind of alarm." As he grabbed her arm, Gwen started to balk. The fingers on her arm tightened and pulled her closer.

"Farrow isn't playing games," he said in a soft voice that frightened her more than an angry, loud one might have. "After Farrow was booked, a bomb was found in your father's golf bag."

Stunned, she needed a moment to register what he'd said. Her eyes snapped to meet his. "My God. That stubborn old coot," she murmured about her father. "He should be in protective custody."

"That's an understatement."

"But you can't possibly believe that Fred—" She sent him a troubled look. "Fred is a friend of the family."

He arched a brow as if he found that questionable.

"He's a friend of part of the family, of mine and Trish's," she corrected.

"Yours more than your sister's from what I've been hearing."

She drew an exasperated breath. "You're nitpicking, Sergeant. He didn't deserve—"

Roughly he grabbed her upper arms and forced her to face him. "Listen. We don't know what the person looks like who might carry out the threat. It could be anyone."

She stared into eyes so serious that they tempted her to sway closer to him for whatever protection he could offer. Instead she struggled to comprehend what he was really saying to her. "You believe one of our friends could be—"

"It's just a possibility that we have to consider. John Farrow is a persuasive man. He knows how to reach and manipulate people."

She shook her head. "No. I don't believe that. And if you think Fred would—"

"He doesn't see eye to eye with your father, does he?"

"Neither do I most of the time. Am I a possibility, too?"

"Hell, no. But you and I wouldn't be going through this charade if we didn't have to consider everyone but your immediate family."

"There is such a thing as loyalty."

"Loyalty can be bought."

Gwen heard a hardness in his voice, a cold hardness, a telltale hardness and considered the smidgen of information she had about his background. A loner wouldn't believe too many people could be depended on. "This is so ridiculous that it's almost laughable. I'm not going to give it another thought. Fred isn't any danger to anyone but himself," she insisted. "And I have too many other things to think about."

"Learning to listen might be one of them. I told you to stay back at the house."

Gwen whipped back and faced him. Too many walls were closing in on her. Frustrated, she didn't know how to explain that to him. "I know you don't want to listen to this. But *I'm* responsible for myself. I agreed to let you guard me. But I decide what I do. And if I make a mistake, that's *my* fault, not yours." She pushed a hand hard at his chest to place more distance between them.

He didn't give her an inch. Anger rose as he yanked her close again. "You won't make a fatal mistake. I won't let you."

Jack watched her eyes darken to a stormy blue that threatened of a coming tempest. A soft, strangled sound slipped from her as she shoved impatiently at his shoulder, then brushed past him.

He didn't try to stop her. A warm summer breeze whirled around him, as if urging more distance between them.

He knew enough to stay detached. Years of experience had taught him not to get too involved with people. He did his job and left. At least he always had. But this time something was different. And that something was a tall, fiery-looking woman whose smile flashed without hesitation.

He was definitely in more trouble than he'd thought, more trouble than he'd been in at any other time during his police career. No gun barrel was pointed at him, no perpetrator was threatening. She was doing what no other person had—scaring the daylights out of him by stopping his breath with the same unexpected excitement of a stakeout when confrontation was close at hand.

"Hell, what happened?" Earl asked, approaching him, his gaze fixed on Gwen as she stormed toward the house.

"The princess wants me beheaded."

His attempt at humor fell flat. Looking baffled, Earl frowned curiously at him.

Jack wasn't looking for a response. He knew the score too well. Jack Mallory didn't have the right credentials or the right background for John Austin Ashcroft's daughter. He didn't even know who his father was.

Fuming, needing to regain some kind of grip on her life, Gwen wasn't certain who she was angrier at, him or herself.

By the time she reached the living room, family members were already gathered at the table for dinner. Heads turned, eyes riveted on her.

"We've been waiting for you and your fiancé," Ardelle chided.

"He—" Gwen's voice faltered as a warm hand touched the small of her back. She drew a quick breath, too aware of how gentle his touch felt now in comparison to when he'd gripped her arm only minutes ago.

As Jack smiled down at her, she saw none of the same amiableness reflected in his eyes. Performance time, he was reminding her. She stifled her annoyance for the sake of their masquerade. Dinner was going to be a fiasco, she thought. All the world's a stage, she told herself as they were seated.

Glued to her side, her Mr. Wonderful flashed his rarely seen knock-your-socks-off smile at her and then set out to charm Ardelle to a state of blushing.

Head tilted, chin raised to the perfect angle, her older sister launched into an inquisition. "What of your formal education, Jack?"

Raising his eyes from his plate, he sent her a humbly pained expression. "Lacking, I'm sorry to say. I didn't have your advantages," he added with a casual backhand sweep at his surroundings.

"Self-made men are to be admired," her father cut in to end questions about Jack's past.

Seeming to acquiesce, Ardelle smiled sweetly at her father. "Yes, of course," she responded, her grudging tone trailing off as her attention shifted to the slice of Moroccan pigeon pie on her plate. "And are you comfortable in your room?"

"It was a pleasant surprise to see an El Greco."

Her fork poised in midair, Gwen nearly choked on a mouthful of pie. What did a Chicago cop know about El Greco? She eyed him suspiciously. Smiling, holding his wineglass before him, he wore his new coat of riches convincingly. Gwen thrust her fork into her

dinner. She would bet he was a superb poker player—
great at bluffing.

With a family as tough to win over as hers, Gwen
would become a spinster if she weren't careful, Jack
thought, escaping the dinner table with the excuse that
he needed to make a business call. He doubted few
men ever passed the Ashcroft interrogations.

Stepping into the kitchen, he eyed a hearty plate of
mashed potatoes and gravy in front of Earl. "How did
you get that?" he murmured when Hillary's back was
to them.

Earl raised only his eyes from his plate. "It's left-
overs."

His stomach rolling enviously at the sight of rare
roast beef, Jack snitched a sliver of it from Earl's
plate. "Is everything calm outside?"

"Nothing going on," he mumbled with his mouth
full.

"I got a list from Ashcroft of the workmen and the
caterers. Check them out. Tomorrow, I'll get a guest
list from Trish Ashcroft."

Scooping up a mound of mashed potatoes, Earl
answered, "Sounds good to me."

"I hope you're enjoying yourself," Jack quipped.

Earl gave him a closed-lipped chipmunk's grin and
a nod, looking quite relaxed for a man whose job en-
tailed risking his life.

Stepping outside, Jack couldn't shake a caged sensation. He'd feel more relaxed in a dark alley pursu-
ing a criminal than he felt in that quiet, elegant house.

* * *

Gwen awoke with a dull, throbbing headache the next morning. She took two aspirin, blaming her discomfort on a restless night spent trying to make sense of what had become a disturbing puzzle—namely Jack Mallory.

Stepping out of the bathroom in her underwear, she heard a soft rap before her bedroom door opened.

Dressed for the tennis game Gwen had promised her the night before, Trish was beaming. "What a stitch dinner was," she said as she charged into Gwen's bedroom. "Though I have to admit, one bite of that pigeon pie was enough for me—yuck! I stuck with the chicken."

"I'm glad you thought it was entertaining." Gwen dug into a dresser drawer for her shorts and a polo shirt.

"You didn't think it was hilarious?"

"Ralston kept pushing food around on his plate and acting like he expected something to start moving. And he didn't even try the pigeon pie." Gwen noted Trish's smile had faded and given way to a frown. "And Ardelle played Perry Mason." She dropped her shorts to the nearby vanity chair. "Justin was the only male I brought home who didn't have to endure the third degree," she went on, yanking the white shirt over her head. "But then Ralston introduced me to him, didn't he?"

"Oh, Gwen, don't think about him," Trish said, predictably trying to avoid anything unpleasant. "Jack is nothing like him."

Gwen was silent, preoccupied with trying to find her way into her shirt.

"Weren't you surprised though?"

"About what?" Gwen mumbled from under her shirt.

"Jack," her sister firmly announced. "He fits in so well. It felt like he was part of the family." Enthusiastically she summed up her feelings. "I like him."

Gwen finally popped her head through the neck of her shirt. "You're getting confused. Don't forget, none of this is real." She said the words as much for herself as for her sister.

Trish frowned back at her. "I already did forget."

"Well, now I'm reminding you again—it's a play, a drama. He won't be around for long." Gwen wiggled into her shorts. She was alert to Trish's silence. "What's wrong now?"

"I was going to ask you that," she said, looking puzzled. "Did something happen between you two?"

When had her little sister learned to read her so well? Gwen bent forward to retrieve a sneaker from under the bedspread. "He's confusing."

Dangling her sneaker, she cringed at how obviously defensive her tone was and dodged Trish's stare. But Jack was confusing. She couldn't forget the smiles he had flashed at her during dinner, the caress of his knuckles across her cheek, the warmth of his breath when he'd pretended to whisper sweet nothings in her ear. And, damn, she couldn't forget the feelings he'd so effortlessly stirred within her. "Come on," she urged, heading toward the door. Suddenly the idea of

whacking a tennis ball as hard as she could seemed
particularly appealing.

Jack spent the morning watching her play tennis
with her sister. Pure agony was the best way to de-
scribe it. Her dancing had merely unnerved him. Desire so strong he wanted to groan hit him as he watched
her body respond to each volley, her thighs tightening
below the high-cut white shorts, her breasts straining
against the soft white shirt, her face glowing from the
exercise.

Afterward, perspiration bathing her face, she appeared more relaxed than she had when she'd charged
past him earlier. As she strolled toward him now,
swinging her racket, she smiled. "Want to play a set?"

Jack couldn't help grinning at how ridiculous the
offer sounded to him. "I don't play."

"Not anything? Or just not tennis?"

"Only what I can win."

"You evade wonderfully," she said, with a blunt
edge. "Let's not forget how you deliberately disappeared so quickly after dinner last night, leaving me to
answer all the questions about you like some fall guy."

"You watch too many cop movies on television."
But meeting her steady, unflinching stare, it hit him—
hard—all that he'd been fighting from the beginning:
He would have been attracted to her at any time, anywhere.

She was his type. Feisty, independent, and definitely sexy. He could see her standing on his sailboat,
her hand wrapped around one of the rigging lines, her

hair blowing in the wind, her skin moist from the lake air. "You got away pretty fast yourself."

"You were watching me?"

"I'm always watching you," he said, disgruntled that there was more truth in his words than she would realize. His preoccupation with her made him uncomfortable. He thought he had learned to keep himself detached. Before he was ten years old he'd been well schooled in the art of detachment as a necessity for self-preservation. Only once before had he been this fixated on a woman. She'd played with him, then scorned him. Once again, he was entering that dangerous domain, he reminded himself.

Gwen couldn't deny the unsteadying effect his answer had on her. Her heart hammering, she faced the facts: He was a man who said more with a look or a touch than some people did with a thousand words. He also fluttered something dangerously close to desire within her.

"Why didn't you stay?" he asked.

Shrugging, she turned away. She didn't tell him that she could only manage so much time with her family before someone inevitably pounced on her for doing something wrong. "My leaving is another story. *You* should have stayed. Ardelle was entertaining. She plays the piano beautifully."

He heard no jealousy in her voice, just an admiring acceptance of a fact.

"I enjoy listening to her, but I have a terrible time sitting still."

He understood that problem. He'd needed to get away, too. At the dinner table, he'd felt the warmth of her and had keyed in on her soft tones in a room filled with more grating ones.

"You did well with them," she said, so seriously that he nearly smiled again. "About the El Greco—"

Jack fished into his shirt pocket for a cigarette. "A sixteenth-century carved wood figure of Saint John."

"I don't want an art history lesson." She swayed back to lean against a white wrought iron bench. "I want to know how you know that?"

"I'm a self-made rich man, remember?"

Exasperation flashed in her eyes. Effortlessly he seesawed annoyance and attraction within her. "Well, you did well through dinner anyway."

He took her words as a compliment. He had known the right fork to use, had managed to hold his own when Ralston had expounded about his new polo pony, and most of all, had understood the quirks of the affluent, who seemed to converse through dinner and say nothing.

"How did you manage it?"

He bent his head to light a cigarette, wondering at her curiosity. Why did she need to know so much? "It's not that difficult a role. The director of a children's home unknowingly started my training when she made me sit in her office one afternoon."

She tilted her head questioningly. "What did you do wrong?"

"A childish prank. At the time, I was willing to give up an hour of playing baseball to see the looks on the faces of the teachers when the sugar they added to their coffee tasted like salt."

"Peck's Bad Boy?"

Smoke hung in the air between them. "They thought so. The director assumed that a ten-year-old boy would press his nose against her office window and longingly watch his classmates playing baseball."

"And did you?"

"No, I wandered around her office, scanning the bookshelves. I found a book about antiques. I saw a type of life I couldn't imagine. It made me realize that things became more valuable as they were passed on from generation to generation." He smiled with the memory. "At that moment, my only possession was a marble that I'd won fair and square from another boy."

"So that book changed you?"

"Knowledge can't change a person's beginnings. Let's just say, it helped me understand better where I fit in." The reminder was for both of them. "Why don't we cut this game," he said softly. Christina had been curious, too. In the beginning, he'd been flattered. In the end, he'd understood that her inquisitiveness about him had been a shallow woman playing out a whim for a new first—an affair with a cop. "I'm better at asking questions than answering them."

"I noticed."

"And you're lousy at taking orders."

She sighed heavily. "You're still angry at me about what happened earlier yesterday evening."

"Seems to me, you were the one who was angry." He'd known other women more beautiful and less challenging. Maybe that was part of the reason why he felt so strongly about her. She challenged him constantly.

Head bent, she slipped the tennis racket into its case. "What do you miss most of all about being away from home?" She couldn't say exactly why she'd asked him that, except since she'd be spending so much time with him—more time than she was comfortable with—she wanted to know him better.

"Sailing." As her eyes widened with surprise, he qualified, "Not yachting. A sailboat."

"What else?" she urged.

He sensed she was trying to find common denominators. He could have told her there weren't any. "Pizza." He decided it was a safe response. "I miss pizza."

"No anchovies?" she said, questioning in a way that asked for his agreement.

He could have lied but saw no harm in the truth. A lot of people shared a love for pizza without anchovies. It didn't mean they were soul mates. "No anchovies," he confirmed.

The smile in her eyes rushed down to her lips. "Me, too," she said, in a tone that registered her pleasure.

It doesn't mean anything, he wanted to say. Not anything.

"If you don't like tennis, what do you play?"

As she bent down to reach her bag, Jack moaned silently as a very seductive backside was aimed at him. "Baseball," he answered, amazed his voice still sounded steady.

Straightening, she zipped up her tennis racket and took a step toward him. "There's a game today."

He shot her a baffled look. It wasn't her words so much as the fact that she seemed to keep close tabs on the local team. "Yeah, I know. How do you?"

Delight sparked another wider smile. "You are a snob," she chided lightly.

"Baseball's not exactly a cultural event."

"Oh, and I suppose tennis is?" she said slowly, reaching for his wrist to check the time.

A touch, a simple touch, left a tingly sensation rushing through him.

Spiky dark lashes shadowing her face lifted quickly to pin him with a wide-eyed stare. "If we hurry, we could make the game." Not waiting for his answer, she turned toward the house, appearing oblivious to the chaos she'd stirred within him. "I'll even buy you a hot dog."

He stood still, following her with his eyes as she walked away. He had to drag his gaze away from the gentle sway of her hips, when she glanced back. "You don't want one?" she asked before reaching for the doorknob.

He shook his head, slowly, meaningfully. "If I take you—" He paused and forced her eyes to meet his again. Deliberately he let the words linger between them for a long moment. "If I take you, I buy."

Her teeth tugged on her bottom lip as if she were considering what wasn't being said. "I'll be ready in ten minutes."

"He's going to strike out," she told him between bites of a hot dog as the baseball game went into extra innings. Hunched forward, her eyes glued to the field, she winced as the batter nearly drilled himself into the ground. "Why did he swing?" she asked to no one in particular. "Keep your eye on the ball."

As she yelled, he watched the play of emotions on her face. Her enthusiasm was addictive; he felt it constantly with her. She did nothing halfheartedly. And as his eyes clung to her hair—sunlight shimmering on it, highlighting the lighter strands woven into the fiery ones—he suddenly yearned to learn if that was true in everything she did.

"Who got you interested in baseball?" he asked when they were inching their way through the crowd toward the parking lot.

Pressed close, she peered at him over the rim of her sunglasses. "Uncle Waldo. He took me to my first game when I was six."

Jack held his fingers lightly on her arm, keeping her near. "Do you ever see the infamous uncle?"

"All the time. He and I are bowling buddies."

Jack swiveled a quick look at her. "You're kidding me."

"About what?"

He didn't release his grip on her as they reached the car and he unlocked the door. "You bowl?"

She clucked her tongue at him, as if he were a child who had a lot to learn, before sliding into the car.

"Hundred-and-fifty average," she said when he was behind the steering wheel.

As Jack switched on the ignition, he caught a glimpse of her crossing her legs. Long and tan, they enticed almost as much as the hint of lace peeking out from the bottom of her shorts.

Quickly he shifted gears and backed up, needing to drive to keep his hands busy, to keep from reaching for her.

## Chapter Five

If he was feeling restless and edgy, that was an occupational hazard, Jack decided later that evening. If he was attracted to her, that was normal. She was a beautiful woman. But there wouldn't ever be anything else between them. Gwen Ashcroft didn't belong with a cop. He wouldn't have even met her, wouldn't be with her now, if it wasn't for his job.

Seeking a quiet spot to retreat to, while Gwen was caught in a dinner-table conversation with Ardelle, Jack wandered into her father's library. Last night he'd strolled through the dark house and into the library for a book. The wide selection had been too exciting to resist.

He slid another book from one of the shelves for reading later, then grabbed the newspaper. He had too many addictions, he thought, including one for crossword puzzles.

Slouched in a chair, he caught himself listening for the soft sensuous sound of Gwen's voice. He cursed and lowered his head to concentrate on the puzzle.

"So, you're a crossword freak."

He barely kept from jumping. How could a woman who could create and control pandemonium in a roomful of people with her unexpected remarks be so damn quiet when she moved?

Seeing his hard stare, Gwen halted in mid-stride, as if uncertain about taking another step closer. "Sorry. I didn't mean to scare you."

He held his scowl for a second longer, as if the idea was too distasteful.

As he bent his head again, she strolled closer. "Do you do those all the time?"

"Occasionally." Any chance he might have had of concentrating on the newspaper was shot, as she stopped behind his chair and her fragrance hovered over him. "They break the boredom of stakeouts."

She peered over his shoulder at the spaces still empty. "That's ecdysiast."

"A stripteaser? Are you sure?"

"She's a dancer, isn't she?" When his eyes met hers, she laughed because he looked so serious. "Sort of."

As she stepped away, he drew in her scent. He wondered if a fragrance, like a thought, could be imprinted in the mind to linger and haunt a person. If so, he was in for trouble in the future.

Circling the room, she paused before the bookshelves. Noticing the empty slot on one shelf, she looked over her shoulder at him, zeroing in on the leather-bound book that he'd decided on for his evening's reading. Keats. Never would she have guessed that he liked to read poetry.

When she said nothing, Jack shifted uncomfortably, imagining that she was questioning his reading tastes. "What brought you in here?" he asked her.

Gwen leaned back against the bookshelves, facing him. "My sister is angry at me, as usual. And she will probably share her annoyance with my father. And he will probably remind me that she only means well."

She turned back toward the bookshelves to grab a book, wishing now that she hadn't come in. She wasn't as immune to him as she had believed. "I'd like to go to the dance studio early in the morning," she said, glancing back.

As he moved toward her, she fought the tensing within her, the thrill slithering over her.

When he stopped, he stood practically on top of her. As he placed a palm on the bookshelf near her shoulder, she was trapped by more than just a strong, masculine body. She was trapped by her own fantasies of him.

"Why did you really come in here?"

She placed a hand on his chest to keep some distance between them. "To talk."

Lightly, he cupped her chin and forced her to meet his gaze. She felt him delving inside her, searching to see beyond what was visible. "Try again," he whispered, bringing his face closer to hers.

She could feel the heat of his breath, smell the life in him, almost imagine his taste.

Her heart was beating hard when his mouth captured hers. There were no illusions of gentleness in his kiss. As he twisted his lips against hers, she tried to tell herself that she wasn't feeling the earth moving. But something as near to that rocked her. He took a deep, full taste of her as if to force a coil of longing around both of them. But it wasn't necessary.

With a will of its own, her body leaned even closer into the warmth of his. She heard his low groan, and felt her own silent one. He was used to weaving a spell over a woman, she realized. Other men also possessed that power, but other men didn't wreak havoc on every sense of control within her. Even as she fought for some semblance of sanity, something exploded within her.

When she coiled her arms around his neck and pressed against him, his mouth became gentler, its touch savoring and almost reverent. A madness skittered through her. She knew she was feeling too much, too quickly. But she couldn't stop what he was stirring within her.

She strained against him, feeling his heat and hardness. She murmured something. She thought it was a protest, but even she wasn't sure. A touch of panic seized her. She didn't want an involvement. She was barely recovered from the last one. And even as a slow-moving ache gnawed at her, she knew the insanity of letting the moment go too far. Somehow, she tore her mouth free from what it wanted. Somehow, she wedged a hand between them and pushed herself away. Somehow, she did it before losing all will to stop him.

She didn't give either of them a chance to say more. Quickly she slipped beneath his arm. She wanted to put distance between them. The accelerated beat of her heart sent her flying toward her room. They were from two different worlds; he'd said it with disgust. Annoyed, she rushed up the stairs, too aware he'd shaken hers.

Gwen decided to stay home the next day. If she didn't leave her room, she wouldn't see him, she reasoned. She spent the morning cleaning out a closet that she'd avoided even looking in for the past three years.

As she smoothed out a crumpled pink hat from college days, she tried to rationalize what she was feeling. While the passion she'd felt could be accounted for, she was terrified of the other emotions he so effortlessly stirred. She liked him. She really liked him. But she shouldn't have let him kiss her. God, why had she done such a foolish thing?

She bunched the hat and tossed it back into a box. She hadn't kissed him. He'd *taken* the kiss.

*Liar,* her mind screamed back at her. If there was one thing she was known for—even to a fault—it was her honesty, especially about herself. She couldn't deny that she had been willing. Almost from their first meeting, she'd wondered what his kiss would be like.

Now she knew. It had been a seduction that had left her reeling. It had made her think of stormy days and dangerous winds. It had insisted that she yield beneath its force. And all she could think about was what would happen if he kissed her again.

Unable to be alone and not think about him, by midafternoon she left her room. A passing inquiry to Detective Lyndon about Jack relaxed her. Since she'd notified Jack early in the morning that she was staying home, he'd driven to his apartment to pick up his mail.

The information made her think of how much she was upsetting his life—no sailing, no pizza. It seemed fair though, she thought. With one kiss, he'd wreaked havoc on hers.

"I'm too impulsive," she said, wandering into the living room. She directed her annoyance with herself at the wedding presents stacked on the mahogany buffet table in the living room.

Trish was there. Thank-you notes for shower gifts were strewn out on the desk before her. She stared at Gwen in puzzlement.

"I am," Gwen said, looking back at her sister. "I'm much too impulsive."

Trish gave a noncommittal shrug. "Why are you suddenly questioning it?"

Gwen fingered a ribbon on a package. "I don't always make wise decisions."

"Nobody *always* makes wise decisions, but you certainly do more than most."

What would Trish say if she knew that the sister she depended on—the sister who, despite a flighty manner, usually was levelheaded—stood one kiss away from giving in to lust? That's exactly what it was, Gwen reasoned. She was lusting for him, probably because he was different—tougher, a touch brooding, an unfamiliar man for the daughter of Ashcroft. She knew nothing of his world, and delicate prodding had revealed that he had bitter memories linked to hers.

"There you are," Ardelle called out from the archway.

Gwen tensed, tempted to charge past her, but the coward's way had never suited her.

"I've been looking for you. I knew something wasn't quite right. Just what is going on?" she asked, reaching forward and lifting Gwen's left hand in the air. "Where is your engagement ring?"

"My—"

"It's unseemly for you to say he's your fiancé and not be wearing a diamond when we go to Aunt Ursula's party."

Gwen silently groaned. "My diamond is—" Nervously she toyed with her belt, then made much about smoothing out the bottom of her yellow tunic top. People said she was quick-witted. She prayed they were right. "He bought it a size too large. It's at the jewelers." Gwen dared a look at Ardelle.

Her frown eased a fraction. "But you will have it for the party, won't you?"

Gwen relaxed, knowing that her explanation had been accepted. "I doubt it."

"Gwen, this isn't a subject open for discussion. You must be wearing that ring by then. People will think it peculiar if you aren't."

Gwen was tempted to remind her that what other people thought wasn't high on her list of important things. Instead she nodded obediently to avoid any more confrontation. "I'll talk to Jack."

\* \* \*

She pleaded a headache to avoid the dinner table. But her spineless behavior didn't sit well with her. While she might want to go on avoiding him, she couldn't continue to avoid her responsibility to her students.

The recital was coming up too soon for her to be hiding in her bedroom. She'd always been competitive in ways her family had never understood. She'd never cared if someone was wearing a dress that cost more or owned a more expensive car or had enjoyed a more lavish vacation. But she viewed difficulties as a challenge. She never shied from them. She confronted them head-on. And at the moment, she deemed Jack Mallory both difficult and challenging.

She would set him straight when she saw him. All she had to do was formulate a plan. As she reached the bottom of the stairs, she saw him standing near the door waiting for her. Her mind went blank the moment he smiled.

She caught herself just before returning the smile, and looked down, feigning concern with something in her purse.

"Headache better?" he asked, when she met him at the door.

"It's gone."

Her pulse scrambled as he caught her chin and held her face still. She didn't want to look into his eyes. She was such a terrible liar.

"If you're going to say it was a mistake, I know it."

She felt his breath fluttering across hers as a reminder of the kiss. She nearly sighed when his fingers grazed her jaw.

"If you're going to tell me to forget it, I can't."

Her pulse jumped like a warning. "I don't want involvement," she said, not too steadily.

He toyed with a strand of her hair. "Yeah, I know."

Gwen slanted a wary look up at him.

He smiled in a slow way that seemed to mock both of them. "Neither do I."

What was he doing to her? she wondered.

"But people don't always get what they want."

His voice was too soft, too compelling. She couldn't have responded even if she'd wanted to. A shiver slithered across her flesh. And as his head dipped and his mouth lightly brushed hers with a quick kiss, she wondered if she would ever come up with a plan to stop him.

Half an hour later at the studio, tension still tightened Jack's shoulders as he stood outside her office. He was decades past the age of infatuation. There had been casual affairs during the past twenty years, but not until his thirtieth birthday had he thought about love. That was when he'd met Christina. He'd been vulnerable, grieving over the death of a good friend. And he'd fallen hard for her. But it only took a few short months for reality to set in. He let go the youthful dream of finding a special woman, having a wife and a family.

And he hadn't celebrated a birthday since.

But suddenly he wasn't so certain that love was something for other people to feel and not himself.

Jamming a hand in his pocket, he strolled closer to her office door and eavesdropped on Gwen and her assistant. They were discussing a possible last-minute revision in the recital program. One of their soloists, an eight-year-old named Mandy, wasn't feeling well.

Certain she was safe, he wandered down the hall to the reception area. As he double-checked the locked doors, he squinted at a dark blue Ford in the parking lot. Behind the steering wheel was a bald man. Jack noted the license number then walked to the telephone.

He learned that the car belonged to a Frank Everett. "What about a rap sheet?" he asked, stretching the cord to look back out the window.

Only a minute had passed, but the guy was gone.

He felt a sharp twist in his gut and hit the hallway skidding. As the door of Gwen's office opened and her assistant strolled out, he saw the chair behind Gwen's desk was empty. "Where is she?"

"Checking costumes."

"Where?"

Startled, the woman reared back. But at the moment, Jack didn't care if she thought he was a madman.

"In the basement," she said, taking several steps back and pointing toward the end of the hall at a stairway.

Nerves coiled tight, he was at the bottom step within seconds. He only glanced at the fire exit. Running, he focused on the end of the corridor. As he rushed around the final corner toward the storage room, he saw Gwen sorting through a rack of costumes. A man stood in the doorway with his back to Jack.

Jack wasn't asking questions first. He plowed into the man's back and sent him tumbling past Gwen and into the closet.

Gwen gasped and swayed back against a wall. This couldn't be happening, she told herself even as she stared at Frank Everett sunken into a bed of costumes. As Jack lunged toward him, she snapped herself into action. "I know him," she yelled.

His eyes swept over her as if needing reassurance that she wasn't hurt.

"His daughter is one of my students." She would have laughed at his perplexed frown were it not for the paunchy man in the closet. An ostrich-feather stole draped his bald head. Gwen wondered how she would explain her overzealous bodyguard. "Oh, Frank." She stepped closer with genuine concern, but he appeared more bewildered than hurt.

Beside her, Jack looked wary and surprisingly a touch embarrassed. She guessed Detective Jack Mallory hated making mistakes and hated even more having to admit to them.

Still, he did the gentlemanly thing. He leaned forward to offer Frank a hand.

Panic widened Frank's eyes. Recoiling, he scooted on his bottom to press his back against the wall. "What's the matter with you? Are you crazy?"

Jack's apology came out easier than Gwen had expected. "Hey, I'm sorry." His smile flickered. "Come on. Let me give you a hand."

At Frank's sidelong glance at her, Gwen smiled in reassurance. "He's really not crazy."

She ignored Jack's stinging look. As he pulled Frank to a stand, Gwen nonchalantly slid the ostrich-feather stole off his shoulder. "You are all right, aren't you?" she asked, preparing to make the best of an awkward moment. Receiving his nod, she gestured with a flare of her hand toward Jack and made her announcement. "This is my fiancé." Nothing but the truth would have made sense, Gwen realized. "He's—he's mildly jealous."

"Mildly?"

Gwen guessed that he thought she was crazy, too, to be in love with such a madman.

Remembering his role, Jack gave a negligent shrug and played the infatuated fool with style. "Love's new to me," he said, draping an arm around Gwen.

Frank grinned suddenly and patted him on the shoulder. "I understand. Love makes a man crazy sometimes," he said, with a sympathy that made Gwen want to punch them both.

Before the situation got out of hand, she eased herself from Jack's embrace and steered Frank toward an adjacent room to make sure he was all right.

"We're just lucky the man has eight children and is used to a life of surprises," she said minutes later when she joined Jack in the hallway.

"What the hell was he doing here so early?" he asked, still sounding mildly annoyed.

"He wanted to talk to me before he went to work."

While they climbed the stairs, he closed the inches between them and slipped a hand around her arm. "Why didn't he come in the front door?"

Gwen counted to five. She would be patient and calm. She wouldn't respond to his irritation. She believed that he was feeling foolish, his ego ruffled. "Frank is a maintenance man for all of these buildings, so he has a key to the fire doors. Since that's the way he always comes in to do his job, I suppose he thought he'd just come in that way now too."

"What did he want?"

She noted that suspicion still colored his voice. "He wanted to talk about his daughter's lessons. He's a proud man. I had to do some convincing to get him to agree that his daughter could keep taking her lessons."

He reached out and caressed strands of her hair before she could stop him. "You're a good teacher. Why wouldn't he want her to take lessons from you?"

His compliment sent a ripple of pleasure sweeping through her. "His daughter's weekly lessons are free. He can't pay," she explained. "But that doesn't mean his daughter shouldn't have the opportunity to dance. I want to offer anyone who wants it a chance to learn the joy of dancing, so I contacted the city park director. She told me of some children who would be interested." At his puzzled look, she smiled. "My sister doesn't understand, either. Ardelle thinks I should close the studio. She's been campaigning for months to get me to do it. It's beneath an Ashcroft to own a dance studio, especially one that gives free lessons."

He urged her toward her office, touching her for no reason except the assurance that she was beside him and safe. "And what do you say to Ardelle?" Jack didn't really have to ask. He'd already learned she didn't like people telling her what to do.

She saw the hint of a grin curving his lips. How in such a short amount of time had he understood her so well that he knew exactly how she would react? "Before I left for Europe, I considered giving it up," she said, drawing a surprised frown from him. "I thought that my rebellious nature had taken over again. I tend to do things just to oppose what I don't like. But while I was away, I missed the children." She preceded him into her office. "Though no one expects me to stay with this, I know I'm not giving it up."

Jack stopped in the doorway and wondered how her family couldn't know the futility of trying to change her mind about anything.

Reaching her desk, she took a calming breath. She needed conversation constantly to keep dangerous thoughts about him at bay. Even now she felt too much excitement, and he wasn't even touching her. Feeling desperate to be alone, to have time to think clearly, she glanced at the clock to signal him to leave. "It's going to be a long day."

"I'm not going anywhere."

She cocked her head questioningly. "Do you plan on staying here?"

All he could remember was how scared he'd been for her earlier. He'd seen the man and the threat had seemed too real. Never had he known such fear for another person. Never had he felt so encumbered by his own emotions, so desperate to protect someone.

As he crossed to her, Gwen told herself she wanted to end whatever was happening between them. She didn't want to be hurt again.

He stopped before her desk and leaned forward, setting his palms on it. "I plan on staying right here."

The softness of his voice swirled around her like a warm caress. She held her breath as he leaned his face closer. She expected his kiss.

Instead he gave her that infuriatingly slow smile of his that she was becoming too familiar with. Gwen drew a quick shaky breath as he turned away and sauntered to settle on a chair in the corner. She doubted she would get anything accomplished with him so near, with him watching her, with him making her ache for that damn kiss.

By midmorning Jack had moved to four different rooms. Grand Central Station wasn't as busy as her dance studio. Near noon he slouched on a chair in the reception room. With one eye on the door and the other on the sports page, he watched as deliveries were made and children straggled in.

He'd fooled himself into believing everything he felt for her was sexual. He was past looking at her, sizing her up and assessing feminine curves. He saw beyond her soft tanned flesh, the elegant lines of her neck and shoulders, the delicate shape of her nose and mouth. She'd touched something deeper within him, much deeper than a masculine reaction to a beautiful woman.

He was still a little confused by everything he felt. He certainly hadn't expected it. But then Gwen Ashcroft wasn't what he'd expected. No phoniness, no facade. She wasn't shallow or spoiled. She wasn't like any woman he'd ever known before.

Briefly she emerged from one classroom with an armful of costumes and three giggling little girls trailing behind her, and then ducked into another. He folded the newspaper to the crossword puzzle and stayed out of her way.

Preoccupied, Gwen had forgotten that a detective was shadowing her, but she hadn't forgotten about Jack Mallory. He was making her feel too much. That terrified her. She was afraid. She admitted it. She was afraid to let her heart open to a man again.

She raised her chin as a fresh wave of determination drifted over her. She wouldn't let herself get carried away by romantic notions because of a few kind words or gentle caresses or a kiss that seemed imprinted in her mind. She wouldn't let her heart be broken again. Feeling a touch out of sorts, she plunged herself into work. She maintained a harried pace, attending to details for the recital, keeping herself too busy to think about him. It wasn't until her stomach growled that she realized she'd forgotten about lunch.

Without a glance at him, she hurried into her office. One look at her desk, and every stupid thought of resisting him was swept away.

Set in the middle was a white bag from a nearby sandwich shop. Beside it, in a glass of water, was a single wildflower. As she inhaled the sweet fragrance, a girlish thrill rippled through her. Other men had sent her bouquets of roses that had meant worlds less to her. You weaken me, she mused.

Despite the morning havoc, the afternoon passed smoothly. As her youngest students filed out, proudly carrying their kelly green elf costumes, she strolled to the reception area, expecting to see Jack patiently waiting. At the sight of an empty chair, she frowned, wondering where he was.

She handed Carrie an armful of music sheets for the different dance routines, then went to the recital room to look for him.

She'd never wondered before where any man was. When she'd been going with Justin, she'd accepted that he wouldn't be around that much. With the symphony, he traveled often. But not once when he'd been gone, had she given thought to where he was or what he was doing.

Be logical, she chided herself. Jack's job was to guard her. She was only wondering where he was, because she wasn't supposed to go anywhere without him. That made sense, she decided. But she had to admit, she wasn't just wondering. She was worrying. What if there's been a confrontation? What if he's outside, lying hurt in the alley?

Less steady than she wanted to be, she paused in the doorway and scanned the room quickly. Relief floated over her as she saw him.

Slouched against a wall, his arms folded across his chest, he watched the cleaning crew energetically scrubbing the floor.

Feeling like an idiot, she strolled toward him.

Though she wasn't in his line of vision, he jerked, snapping toward her. "Damn, don't be so quiet."

She looked at his hand, fisted and ready, and laughingly raised a warding-off one to him. "You're jumpy," she said in a deliberately lighthearted tone meant to ease away his frown.

Glancing quickly back at the cleaning crew, he crossed the room with her. She felt tension in the fingers circling her arm and urging her into the hallway. Because he looked so serious about three men who were close to retirement age, Gwen couldn't resist a teasing attempt to ease the tension. "Did you strip-search them?"

He sent her a withering look. Struggling to abate a laugh, she stepped out of the room ahead of him. Sometimes he could look so serious, almost stern. She knew he must be a good cop—he was so conscientious. She gave little thought to danger when he was near, guarding her. It seemed ironic that she could feel safe and in jeopardy with him at the same time.

When they passed her office, she thought about the flower. Constantly he stirred mixed feelings in her. Annoyance and attraction. Exasperation and pleasure. She'd been foolish to believe she could ignore him and what he made her feel. She doubted if anyone could ignore him once he decided to do differently.

Nearing the exit, she tried to sound casual, but nothing would stop the pleasure still coursing through her. "Thank you for lunch." She paused to hold down an absurd giveaway smile. "And the flower."

"A long-stemmed rose would have suited you better," he said softly. He rolled up the newspaper in his hand and reached around her to open the door. Jack hadn't considered why he'd given in to a romantic notion except that he'd wanted to please her.

With her near him now, he allowed himself to admit to what he'd pushed to the back of his mind. He had wanted her to know she meant more to him than a job. Holding the door for her, he skimmed her arm when she passed him, and he wondered what was the point to anything he wanted if she didn't feel the same unbearable need.

Rush-hour traffic bottled the streets. Concentrating on the cars in front of him, Jack shifted lanes and made the turn onto Lake Shore Drive toward the address she'd mumbled. The smell of lake air hit him soundly. It was like a welcoming. He glanced at the water, gray beneath an overcast sky, and thought of how much time he'd spent on the lake. It was home to him more than his apartment was. For some reason, he felt compelled to see his boat. Whatever might or might not happen between them, he wanted to take her on his boat and have memories of her there. "You don't get seasick, do you?"

Gwen threw him a tough look. "Never."

## Chapter Six

As the wind caught the sails, the hull sped through the water. His hand on the tiller, Jack watched his guest. She looked relaxed. Beautiful. When the sun peeked out from behind heavy clouds, her hair turned fiery beneath the brightness. She looked the way he'd fantasized seeing her ever since their first meeting.

Gesturing with her head, she drew Jack's attention to a sea gull skimming the water in search of food. "Lucky, aren't they? Sea gulls are free," she said as an explanation.

Squinting, he peered at her, concerned at the trace of melancholy he heard in her voice. "So are you."

"Not always." Dimples cut faint lines near her mouth as she gave him a halfhearted smile. "Do you feel free out here?"

He thought her question odd until he considered it. She was right. Freedom was what had lured him to sailing, what made him seek it when troubled. Being alone was something he was used to, but the feeling of loneliness never left him. He'd spent most of his holidays sailing to escape that loneliness, to feel free from it at a time when others were with their families. "You're a smart lady."

She laughed, looking more amused than complimented by his words. "I feel that way about dancing. It takes all my energy, all my concentration. It helps me think less about problems that I can't do anything to change." Leaning over, she stared down at the water. "How did you get interested in sailing?"

"God, don't you get tired of asking questions?"

She returned his smile and sat back again, bending her knees. "Never. Tell me," she urged. "Why sailing?"

He could have tried to dodge her question, but the evasiveness he used to keep a part of himself from other people didn't work with her. He wasn't certain why that was so. "I used to live in Florida," he said, watching the waves. "I was out of high school and drifting when I heard about a deep-sea treasure hunter who needed a crew to sign on for the summer. Harry was his name. He wanted to search for a Spanish galleon that had sunk in the Caribbean. He was a salty old guy who was only comfortable when a boat was rocking beneath him."

Shifting, Gwen propped an elbow on the rail and rested her jaw on her palm. "A good friend?"

"The best." More than a friend, Jack reflected. "At the end of every day, we would sit for hours on the deck, and he would talk. He'd been a cop and had a million stories. I was young and eager to hear them all." He grinned, recalling his enthusiasm during those years. "He would feed me clues from cases." Jack looked up and matched her smile. "I found out I was pretty good at solving them. When we returned to Florida, I joined the police academy."

"What about Harry?"

He paused, releasing his grip on the rigging. "He's dead now. After he died, I moved to Chicago. Great man," he said softly, wondering why he didn't remember those good times more often.

Gwen watched as a peacefulness softened his features. She felt relaxed for the first time in days. She hadn't realized how much she'd needed to get away. How had he known to offer her this? she wondered, leaning back and letting the wind toss her hair.

As he swayed toward her, Jack looked into her eyes. A vibrant green cast mingled in with the blue, reminding him of the water.

"If you could, you would want to be here all the time, wouldn't you?" The sounds of water lapping against the sides of the boat, and canvas flapping in the wind, drowned out her voice.

Crouching before her, he slid an arm around her back. "Not always."

"Not fond of mermaids?"

"No." He leaned in to her. "I have a thing for great-looking legs. And you can't always find them out here."

She stared at his lips, feeling warmed by his smile. Everything about him drew some kind of extreme reaction from her. As she felt his hand on her back, she recalled her anger at its strength when he'd restrained her, and her excitement at its gentleness when he'd caressed her. And how often had she tensed from his cool look, or felt a slithering flush of heat from his warm one?

Something intangible right from the beginning had made her need to get close to him. How could he have become so important to her so quickly? She had no answers about what she felt for him. She only knew she didn't want to be hurt. But how could she ignore the emotions that skittered through her whenever he looked at her or whenever he touched her?

She tried to think but she couldn't. As he scooted her down to the deck with him, her arms coiled around his neck and she felt a willingness overshadowing every other emotion.

Suddenly nothing mattered but the taste of him. Her mouth tingled beneath the intense pressure and clung to his. She'd expected a rough kiss again, but instead found him so gentle she ached from the tenderness. Slow and savoring, his mouth moved over hers, and a need whipped through her unlike any she'd ever known before. She felt his hand roaming over her. Head swimming, she couldn't stop him. Breathless, she pulled him tighter to her, even as she knew how close she was to letting go all reason. But if she didn't stop him, how would she protect her heart?

Even as pleasure rippled through her, fear grabbed hold. She tore her lips from his and steeled herself as much for what she was feeling as to how he'd respond. And achingly she wished that she could trust him. Oh, God, why couldn't she offer her heart again?

Breathing hard, his hand still firm on her thigh, he stared down at her with more understanding than she'd ever anticipated. "It's too late to say you don't feel the same," he whispered, his mouth brushing lightly across hers again. "Too late."

Her heart thudded as if it would burst through her chest.

Jack watched warring emotions cross her face. He'd felt the heat in her. When she pulled back, he sensed she was battling herself more than him. He wanted to drag her against him again and dive his hands into her hair, absorb every sensation, take his fill. He'd relished every second of that kiss. Even now her taste lingered. When his mouth had come down on hers, he'd heard a soft sound, a moan. It had fueled him. And the more she'd responded, the more he'd wanted. He had thought he'd lost that desire, that hunger. He was wrong.

He had no conflict any longer. She was different from other women. She had stirred something within him, had reached the hollowness in his heart, so that even the simplest of life's pleasures had become more satisfying when she was near. That was why he'd brought her to the boat. And he knew that he would never spend another moment on it and not feel her presence there with him.

Clouds still hung heavy in the sky the next morning. Strolling into the quiet kitchen, Jack couldn't decide whether or not he was fooling himself. He'd reasoned that her lack of encouragement was apprehension. She seemed almost frightened of his getting too close, and he wondered why. He could have told her that she wasn't the only one wary. He had his own reasons to be apprehensive. He'd learned his lesson from another woman. But all the reasoning in the world didn't stop him from wanting her.

At the click of the kitchen door, he turned away from the stove to the sight of a sleepy-looking Earl.

Eyes hooded, he yawned. "Am I glad you're awake." Earl let out a huge sigh. "This isn't going to be a good day."

"Is the refrigerator empty?"

"Funny." Earl grimaced at the thick-looking coffee in Jack's cup. "Right before dawn—" He paused and fought with the lid of a cookie canister. "Right before dawn, two of Farrow's men were spotted on the road outside the gate. I called Caulder. The captain has put us on high alert."

Every nerve in Jack's body tensed at the news. The stakes had become so high. He wasn't protecting the Ashcrofts anymore; he was protecting Gwen and her family. And she wasn't going to like him changing her plans about going to the studio, Jack thought with certainty. Hell, she'd put up a stubborn stink about it.

Nervously Gwen fingered the silverware on the buffet table and stared back at her father. After a twenty-minute discussion with him about her plans, she'd finally wangled an agreement out of him. "You will tell Jack that you have no problem with it, won't you?'' she asked, doubting Jack would acquiesce as easily.

As she glanced back over her shoulder, she noticed her father hadn't touched his eggs Benedict. He looked up from the newspaper before him and peered over the rim of his glasses at her. ''I couldn't say that truthfully. I *do* have a problem with it. I'd prefer you didn't want to do this, but I know you too well. The more I argue against it, the more willful you'll get. And in the end, I'll agree.''

Gwen turned away from the buffet table. Balancing a cup of coffee on a saucer, she crossed to him and touched his shoulder. ''Am I so difficult?''

''Difficult?'' He shook his head, a vague smile brightening his eyes. ''No, not difficult. Exhausting.''

''Jack will agree,'' she assured him with more confidence than she felt.

Approaching the dining room, Jack caught her comment and mentally geared himself for more trouble than he'd already anticipated.

At her father's distracted look, Gwen spun around and saw Jack. Her eyes darted uneasily back to her father, before she drew herself straighter and snapped on a smile. If he had had a shield, Jack thought, he couldn't have protected himself from its charm.

''Oh, good, you're awake,'' she said, scooting around the table to the buffet.

As a cop, he was used to observing and seeing behind the masks people donned. Her manner seemed too bright, too enthusiastic. He was certain she was feigning it for his benefit, but why?

In what he viewed as nervousness, she took a bite of a croissant, set it down and picked up the silver coffeepot. "Father and I have been talking." She faced him with the coffee she'd poured.

Warily Jack stared at her smile and the coffee cup she was offering to him like a bribe.

"I need to be closer to the studio to handle last-minute problems. Father's agreed that for a few days, there would be no harm in my staying at my own apartment." She paused and bit into the croissant again, waiting for her verbal bomb to explode.

It took a moment for her words to register. "Your apartment?" he asked incredulously. "You can't stay at your apartment."

"I don't see any problem."

"You don't?" When she tipped her chin up a notch stubbornly, he had to struggle against a desire to shake some sense into her. Instead he swung a disbelieving look at Ashcroft. "You didn't agree with this, did you?"

She jumped in before he could answer. "Jack, don't make it harder on him. No, he doesn't really want me to go," she admitted, giving up her act. "But he understands that I made a commitment to my students."

"That's not my problem. Protecting you is."

She leveled a steady gaze at him that might have nailed a lesser man's back to a wall. "Would you leave another police officer who was depending on you?"

She punched hard and accurately.

"You're with me all the time here," she said in a slow, measured manner as if trying to reason with someone slightly dense. "So what difference does it make if I'm there or here?"

"It makes a big difference."

"Jack." Her voice carried an appeal. "You protect me here, don't you?"

He sensed a trap but couldn't see any way to avoid it. "Yes."

"You'd protect me there, wouldn't you?"

"Yes," he said grudgingly.

She smiled brightly, first at her father then sweeping to Jack. Both men looked uncertain. "Then there's no problem," she said. "I'm going."

As she glided past them, Jack nearly yanked her to a standstill to make her listen to reason. He shot a glare at her father. "She's spoiled."

"Exasperating." The older man grinned suddenly.

Jack found nothing humorous about the moment. "Yeah, that, too."

Swearing, he stormed back into the kitchen, nearly bowling over Hillary, who held a silver tray ladened with homemade muffins. She gave a startled gasp before recovering herself enough to push by him into the dining room. Earl looked up from a plate of scrambled eggs and frowned at him. Jack announced to his friend his latest irritation. "Gwen and I won't be here for the next few days."

Earl dragged his gaze away from his plate. "Where are you going?"

"She wants to stay at her apartment."

"Couldn't you talk her out of it?"

Jack gave him a look of disbelief. "Other than locking her in her room, how do you suggest I do that?

Caulder didn't give an okay to place anyone under house arrest.''

Shaking his head, Earl responded with an amused snort and poked his fork back into the eggs.

On a curse, Jack spun around. What was so damn funny to everyone?

Quieter than usual, she bent forward on the car seat and flicked on the radio. Jack wondered if she felt a need to break the silence between them, but she tuned the music in so low that he heard her soft sigh.

"I know you're not happy about my staying at my place. But I would have had to go there anyway. To pick up a dress." Fiddling with the dial again, she reminded him, "My aunt's party is soon." She settled back, setting her hand on the edge of the open window, and drummed her fingers in time with an upbeat country and western song. "Did Horton bring you a tuxedo?"

Her questioning tone snapped Jack out of a daze. He forced himself to draw his eyes away from a mouth that he knew was soft and sweet. What had she asked him? he wondered, trying to weave his way through muddled thoughts. Tuxedo. Something about a tuxedo.

When he finally offered a nod, she went on, "I can't say I'm eager to see my aunt."

Jack concentrated on the traffic ahead of him. He wondered if he was going mad, but somehow managed to keep up the conversation. "Not one of your favorite relatives?"

"I'll let you judge her for yourself. But don't worry. For one evening, *I'll* protect *you.*"

He doubted anyone could protect him from the heat she stirred so easily with her smile.

He was on a roller coaster, he decided later that day. The moment he passed the doorman and stepped into the marble lobby of her apartment building, his own questionable beginnings slammed back at him.

He strolled behind her into her apartment, not knowing what to expect. Neutral in color except for splashes of orange, it was both modest and grand. The east wall of the living room, clad in marble, reflected a skyscraper view. He contemplated the armless chairs and the settees with their two cushions and wondered where comfort fell on her list.

"Like it?" she asked, smiling.

"Too many windows."

Gwen laughed softly behind him. "But do you like it?"

He squinted at something abstract with rings and chrome that was mounted on one wall near a bonsai plant. "It's—it's different from what I'm used to."

"And you only like what's familiar to you?"

"I'm a simple man," he said, scanning the apartment quickly, making sure it was secure, as well as satisfying his curiosity.

"Odd," she said from the doorway of an adjacent room. "I find you rather complex."

His puzzled look went unnoticed as she entered the other room.

He felt as if he'd entered another world. A lacquered dining room table was mounted on a slab of marble, and on a marble sideboard were crystal globes with stalks sticking out of them. Above them was an abstract painting, splotches of orange that circled something resembling an eye. He walked over to one of the settees and patted a cushion. Hard. The damn thing had no give to it.

He circled back to the windows and stared down at the street. She lived in a world where even the city streets looked clean. He was a fool. All his life, he'd seemed to want what wasn't obtainable. Unobtainable, that's what she was to him. He wanted her because she was like the sun—warm and vibrant, but out of his reach.

"Do you like the view?" she asked.

"I have the same one for a lot less money." Whipping around, he saw that questions clouded her eyes. He could hear her silent words. *Why? Why are you always pushing me away?*

He rubbed his knotting neck muscles. What explanation could he give her for his unreasonable anger? His gut was tight, his desire strong, and an urge to yank her into his arms was too close to the surface for either of them not to feel it. "Let's go." She didn't move, but stunned him by reaching a gentle hand out to him. "It's not your fault. It's mine," he tried to assure her.

"I don't think so," she said weakly.

If he made a move she wouldn't stop him, he realized. Hunger for her whipped through him like an unseen storm. "Dammit, don't you know that I want you? Don't you know how much I want you?'' He spoke the words without thinking; his own voice—softer, huskier—sounded strange to him. He saw the flicker of a smile at the edges of her lips, even as puzzlement still marred her brow.

"We—"

"No," he flared back. "There is no 'we.' I've taken this trip before. It's a dead end," he said, frustrated with both himself and her.

She shook her head. "I don't understand."

How could she? Maybe he hadn't been fair to either of them, he decided. "Ever heard of Christina Bridgemont?"

"The Palm Beach Bridgemonts?"

"That's the family." He swore, feeling trapped by more than just the blue eyes that pinned him. "I was working on a case, investigating robberies in the high rise where she lived. We met, something clicked and I began to see her. It didn't last," he said simply. "She'd never expected it to be more than an amusing adventure." Even now, he felt dumb for ever believing in a future with Christina. He could still hear her laughter as she'd told a friend that she had been the first of her crowd to bed a cop.

How could he have forgotten? Memories only five years old shouldn't have faded so easily. He'd been blinded by one woman's soft smiles and lighthearted ways, and now, for the second time, he could call himself a fool.

"Jack?" A softness whispered in the air to him. "I don't want to go."

He wondered if she had any idea what might lie ahead for both of them. He drew a hard breath, several, stunned that he had to grapple for control not to grab her. Madness, he told himself. He was going mad. He wanted to make love with her. He wanted this woman so much he actually felt himself tremble with longing.

Was she still breathing? Gwen wondered. As his gaze clung to hers, desire crackled in the air between them. After saying those words to her and giving her the gift of trust, did he really expect her to turn away as if nothing had happened?

His eyes swept searchingly over her face, as if trying to see inside her mind. Say something, anything, she wanted to beg, her hand trembling when it touched his cheek. "Say it again," she urged against the corner of his lips.

"What?"

"That you want me."

Rationality didn't matter, he realized. Nothing mattered but the ache to know her intimately and feel all that he'd been fantasizing about from the beginning. Regardless of what the past had taught him about women who lived in palaces, his blood had warmed from the moment he'd met her. He felt a wildness to have her, to know her warm body beneath his hands, to feel it slick with dampness. And he knew logic didn't matter. "Want?" Heat licked at him, quick and intense. "Want?" he repeated on a hard breath, framing her face with his hands. "God, woman, I ache for you."

She heard the torment in his voice. She knew the conflict within herself and him. But with him so close, isolated from everyone but each other, she didn't want to worry about consequences. A sense washed over her of how right the moment was. She placed a hand against his chest and felt his heart pounding in the same quick beat as her own. "You are going to make love with me, aren't you, Sergeant?"

On a moan, he muffled her words with his lips against hers. She was starving for him, she realized, slipping her hands upward from his waist to close around his back. She knew that the most natural moment in the whole day was this one. The most natural place was here in his arms. She explored his face, she measured his shoulders, she grazed his waist. Everywhere, he was strong.

His kisses were rarely gentle. Or forgettable. He invaded, using a kiss as his only weapon, but it was powerful and weakening. As if she'd been running for her life, her heart thudded and blood pounded in her ears. She tried to think, to breathe. She only felt, losing herself in him, her body pressing hard against his as a consuming fire ran rampant through her. She felt hungrier the more she tasted his seduction, the more his lips consumed with a thoroughness that snatched away her breath.

"Soft. You're so damn soft." His mouth drifted over the shell of her ear. "Are you real?" he asked, his breath harsh, as if trying to convince himself.

Oh God, it all had to be real, she thought. If it wasn't, why then did her skin tingle wherever he touched it? Why did her lips burn from his kiss? Why did she feel so heady with sensation that she would follow him anywhere?

Jack felt the desire within her like fire. He'd only dreamed of this willingness. He'd only fantasized of her heat. He'd never allowed himself to really believe anything was possible between them.

But this was only a beginning, he told himself, twisting his mouth across hers. Only a beginning.

He dragged her even closer, curving her softness to him, longing to say poetic words, soft words. But he wasn't a poetic man, and his mind was suddenly too intoxicated by her scent to think clearly.

Whatever he'd expected paled in comparison to the demanding need that was rushing through him. He heard her sigh to his touch, and he was lost to everything but her.

He wanted to give her gentleness, but a need that promised to push him over the edge possessed him as he scooped her into his arms and carried her into the bedroom. When he lowered her to the bed, she pulled him to her, sinking him against her and whispering two words that flamed him even more. "Love me."

In his wildest dreams, he hadn't expected it to be like this. They lay on the bed, their legs tangled, pushing at denim, pressing flesh to flesh.

As her mouth searched his, his met it. As her heart pounded, his raced. He tasted her, spreading nibbling kisses downward, feeling her skin quiver. He touched her, trailing his fingers along her thighs, caressing soft, hot inner flesh, tormenting himself even as he pleased her. Nothing seemed enough. She was seductive, an enticement that was as exotic as it was natural. No sensible thoughts existed in his mind. He only knew he'd longed for her, had ached to make her breathless just like this.

"Jack," she murmured.

He didn't respond. He couldn't speak. He was lost in her. As he touched her with his hand then tasted the same sensitive curves, a mindlessness grabbed hold.

She gave, too, tearing his breath from him. Her hands as eager and greedy as his own, her lips tantalizing then demanding, her tongue taunting his, insisting on a sensual play. She was sweet and wild and absorbing. She was driving him mad, until his touch no longer soothed or stroked.

Rolling her beneath him, he stared down at her, wanting to see her face, to watch her for a second. Her eyes closed, she pressed her head back into the pillow, fiery red hair fanning across the white pillowcase. Then she opened her eyes and he saw the heat of passion in them, heard her sigh of pleasure, felt her tremble beneath the caress of his hand.

As she writhed beneath him, he pulled her arching hips closer. He was beyond anything he'd ever felt before, and he'd long ago given up trying to reason when her legs curled to hug his hips. Breathless, he pressed into her. Flesh blended with flesh, a heat flowing between them. He heard her whimper his name, he felt her fingers cutting into his back, her mouth against his shoulder, and he rode a wave of sensation, floated across it, felt himself drowning beneath it. He gave all that he could, not worrying about tomorrow. It was too far away. All that mattered was now. All that mattered were these moments, frozen forever in his memory.

He had no idea how much time had passed. On a ragged breath, he tightened his hold on her and rolled to his back, keeping her with him. If it had been a mistake, he didn't want to think about it. With her length stretched against him, he was certain of one thing: This was what they'd both wanted.

Gently he sifted his fingers through her hair to find the sensitive spot beneath her earlobe. As she shifted, he nearly groaned when her flesh rubbed his.

"It probably wouldn't be as good the second time," she murmured, just before her tongue began making lazy circles on his shoulder.

He curled his fingers over her thigh. "Probably not."

"Spontaneity has charm." She braced herself over him and kissed his belly. "But, we might—"

"Try again," Jack managed on a quick breath. He wanted control this time. He wanted to savor. He wanted a lover's pace before the heat came. And with one caress, with the expert hand of a magician waving a wand, she invited him to try. She flirted with his control, with tender, soft caresses; with light, nibbling kisses; with the slow, gentle movements of her body. Pushing his head back, he wondered if the pleasure could be more intense. Even now, as he sought the pleasure of her mouth inching downward, he wanted to please her. But blood pounded in his head and through his body. Sanity slipped from his reach. As the ache grew stronger, he challenged himself not to give in to the final release, to the final pleasure, not yet.

## Chapter Seven

No promises, Jack told himself. He wouldn't make any. He wouldn't ask for them.

Sunshine glared into her apartment as he paced about. He scanned his surroundings again and cursed a sensibility that forced him to see their relationship too clearly. He thought the reasonable way to handle everything was to discuss it with her. She was too astute not to recognize the problem that existed between them.

Dressed in jeans and a pink sweatshirt, she tipped her head impatiently. "Come on." She waited in the kitchen doorway. "I'll fix us something to eat."

Because her mood was so bright, and he couldn't stand the thought of snatching away her smiles, he said nothing to break the spell they both were under.

"You can cook?" he asked, following her. As she opened the refrigerator door and bent forward, he watched the denim strain across the tops of her slender thighs.

"There isn't much here," she said, sounding oddly surprised before she flung open the freezer door. "Oh, this might be good."

Jack felt as if she were reaching into Pandora's box. "Don't you know what's in your own refrigerator?"

"Yes and no. When I wrote Trish that I'd be home for her wedding, she promised to stock the refrigerator with food, but she's not too domestic. I'll just heat this," she said, facing him and grinning.

He eyed the white carton with Wong's Chinese printed on the side of it. "For breakfast?"

"Oh, are you one of those people who won't eat anything but cereal and eggs at this time of day?"

He nodded his head. "Yeah, one of those dull people." She laughed—a sultry laugh that slithered over him. "Anyway, I never really developed a liking for Chinese food." Food wasn't on his mind. Nothing. was, except her. He strolled close with intentions of peering at the contents of the container, but her fragrance tempted him more. Bending his head, he kissed the curve of her neck. "What is that?"

"It's good," she assured him, but she squinted as if trying to guess at the contents. "I think it's subgum chicken."

As she looked back in the refrigerator, Jack wondered if there was a fast-food restaurant nearby.

"Eggs. How did I miss these? I have eggs," she said brightly. "Would you like an omelet?"

She looked so pleased to find them, he felt compelled to say yes. "Yeah, that would be okay."

She made a great omelet. Minus the oriental accompaniment, it settled Jack's rumbling stomach. While she cleaned up in the kitchen, he walked back to the living room to telephone Earl.

He heard her humming over the sound of running water while she washed dishes, and he could too easily imagine more moments like this one.

When the water stopped, so did his fantasy. He glanced around him at the high-priced furniture, doubting his annual salary could pay for one roomful of it.

"Ready?" She beamed at him from the doorway.

No, he wasn't, he realized, not wanting to lose the dreamy aftermath of loving her.


Truth will haunt a man. Later that day, when they left the dance studio and stepped outside to pewter clouds threatening rain, his own cloud suddenly descended upon him. He had to be straight with her. He owed her that much. "Are you hungry?"

Her arm on his back, she brushed her hip against his as they walked. "For food?"

He saw the impish sparkle in her eyes and laughed. Had he ever laughed so much before? Would he ever know this overwhelming contentment again in his life? he wondered, as he unlocked the car door for her.

She swayed back against him, her lips brushing his jaw. "If it's food you want, I vote for pizza."

"Pizza it is," he said lightly, but wasn't sure he'd still have any appetite at all once he started talking to her.

"Is this a hangout of yours?" she asked, looking around the small restaurant with its red-and-white tablecloths.

"It's a dive," he admitted over the rumble of thunder outside. "But they serve great pizza."

Balancing a slice on her fingertips, she nodded before chomping down.

Tell her, he railed himself. Don't be so damn gutless. "Listen," he started, then paused to reach for his mug of beer. "We need to talk."

She met his stare and chewed more slowly, worry instantly clouding her eyes. "Why don't I think I'm going to like what you're about to say?"

"Probably because I don't like the fact that I've got to say it." He set down his mug. Didn't she understand the turmoil he could cause in her life? "I really don't know who my father was, Gwen."

"I know. You told me that." She said it so matter-of-factly, he almost believed his background wasn't important. It wouldn't have been if her name weren't Ashcroft, if she didn't have a bloodline that stretched back to the American Revolution. "My mother never even told me his name," he went on, staring down at the pizza untouched on his plate. "Maybe she planned to tell me when I was old enough, but she died when I was three."

He raised his eyes to her face, saw a flicker of uneasiness stir a frowning line between her brows. She wasn't any more comfortable with the conversation than he was. "And then what?" she asked.

"Children's homes, a few foster homes." As she remained silent, he drew a hard breath.

She looked a touch uncertain, almost hesitant. "How did she die?"

"I was told that she was hit by a car. According to a neighbor who had been taking care of me at the time of the accident, my mother was a waitress, a hard worker, battling to make ends meet. When they found her, there was a grocery bag beside her. She'd run out to get milk. For me, I guess."

She stared at him thoughtfully for a long moment. "And there aren't any distant relatives?"

Jack met her stare. "No one."

"So you're the one and only."

He laughed. He hadn't meant to. There was more to tell her, but she had an uncanny way of making him take himself less seriously. *God, woman, what are you doing to me?* He couldn't recall any other time in his life when he'd laughed about his background.

"Is that it?" she asked, looking unfazed by what he'd said.

*No, there's more,* he wanted to say. But he couldn't get the words out as he stared into her too-accepting eyes.

"It's not important, Jack, if you can't trace your ancestors to George Washington's shoemaker. I don't care about any of that."

"Your family will," he felt compelled to remind her.

She shook her head wildly as if to banish his words from her mind. "I don't care. *I* don't care," she repeated firmly. "I just care about you."

He'd never expected those words. He'd never heard them before from anyone. Yet he couldn't go on. He couldn't tell her the rest, knowing that her family would care. They'd care so much that eventually they'd force her to make a choice, one he couldn't ask of her. He couldn't be the reason for more hurt in her life.

Gwen fretted because his troubled frown hadn't disappeared by the time they reached her apartment. She longed for a way to reassure him, but wasn't certain there were words adequate enough. Time, she thought, with the old optimism that had kept her going through other difficult moments. Time will reassure him.

Unlocking her door, she stood still for a long second, certain she was imagining the sight before her. She groped quickly for the light switch on the living room wall. None of this is real, she told herself, desperately.

Red paint dripped down the marble wall from crudely printed letters that spelled out one word: Warning.

She began to tremble, at first with fear, then anger. She swallowed back tears. Reminded of Jack's presence by his hard grip on her arm, she let him propel her toward the wall behind the door.

Frozen to the spot, she steeled herself against returning fear as she watched him slowly work his way through the room, his service revolver in his hand. The threats against her father—like a river branching out— had flowed to reach her.

The moments crept by, agonizingly slow. Panic clawed at her. When he finally reentered the room, she had to fight not to release a sob of relief. Saying nothing, he stopped, used the telephone, then shoved her out the door. She couldn't speak as the danger settled over her with a weight so oppressive she had to gasp to breathe. Someone had known she would be at her apartment. Someone was watching her.

"I called for an investigation squad," he said when they were settled inside the car.

Gwen nodded, fighting the desire to fling herself at him. She was determined to sound strong, but she gripped her purse strap so tightly that the leather cut into her palm. "Now what?"

"We have to wait. Someone will check out the apartment. I'll drive you back to your father's home."

Of course, she realized, that was the reasonable thing to do. But she couldn't go. She knew once she got there, once her family learned what had happened, she wouldn't get free of the house until the whole thing was over. "Jack, not until after the recital."

His head snapped toward her. Even in the darkening interior of the car, she could see the disbelief in his eyes. "Do you understand what's happened here?"

She wasn't stupid or foolish. She didn't want to jeopardize her life or his. But she believed in some simple values like honesty and commitment. She tried to explain, sensing he was at the limit of his patience with her. "Jack, please try to understand. Everything I've ever wanted has been handed to me. My sisters accept that. I can't. I need to be my own person. I need to make my own choices. I need to control my own life."

"No one is trying to take any of that from you," he said angrily.

"I know you aren't, but this recital is important."

"More important than your life?"

"It's part of my life. I can't get this close to proving something, not only to my family but also to myself, just to give it up. Hasn't there ever been anything you really wanted?" She saw a flicker of vulnerability flash in his eyes. He understood. Though he'd swear that his past didn't matter to him, in his youth he must have yearned for a family. She leaned closer on the car seat to touch his forearm. "This is for me. Please," she appealed to him, aware that she would beg if she had to. "Please, help me finish what I started. Don't take it from me."

He was silent. A squad car pulling into the garage brought him to life. Before pushing open the door to leave her, he said one word—an order—"Lock."

Again time was her enemy, passing with excruciating slowness while she waited for him to come back to the car. Finally he opened the door. Only after he switched on the ignition did she speak. "Where are we going?"

"Someplace safe if you insist on staying in the city until after tomorrow."

She wanted to fling her arms around his neck for the gift he'd just given her. She doubted he would ever know how much that concession meant to her. "Where?" she asked, squinting through the rain-splattered window as slanting drops curtained buildings and thundered on the roof of the car.

"My place."

Within minutes he braked in front of a brick triplex in the older part of the near-downtown area. At the flick of a light switch, Gwen realized his apartment was what she'd expected. Comfortable-looking, it was decorated in a no-nonsense manner—shelves filled with books and magazines, and heavily cushioned furniture.

Drenched from running to the building, she tugged at a strand of stringy hair. She heard the roar of the lake nearby despite the wail of the wind and rain.

He raked a hand through his dripping hair, then over his wet face. "There's a clothes dryer in the corner of the kitchen," he said, locking the door behind him and pointing. "You look cold. My robe is in the bathroom."

She looked scared is what Jack really thought. As she hurried to the bathroom, he snatched up the portable phone and strolled to the back porch.

Sitting on a wrought iron chair, he listened to the syncopated beat of the rain for a few minutes before dialing Earl. With the telephone receiver cradled between his jaw and shoulder, he tugged off his wet shirt. "Tell Ashcroft I moved her to someplace safe. My apartment," he said, glancing back at a sound behind him. "Yeah, it's a real mess over there."

She glanced at the aquarium filled with brightly colored tropical fish and then joined him on the porch. Even beneath the mantle of night he could see that she was pale. God, he felt desperate to keep her safe, to ease the worry he saw in her eyes. Yet he couldn't help but wonder if she'd have any reason left to need him once he did all that. "You look better in that than I do," he said, making light of his own insecurity.

Fingering one of the rolled-up sleeves at her wrist, she offered a faint smile. "It's big." Unconsciously he let his gaze drift upward, slowly, over the robe, as she ambled forward. "You called Earl?"

"I didn't want them putting an alert out on us," he said, thinking she looked as if she needed a hug more than anything else. Lightning brightened the sky, illuminating her face in an unearthly glow. Rain pelted harder, duetting with the roar of the water on the shoreline. Standing, he saw her shiver, and drew her to him. "Easy," he soothed, gently stroking her hair.

Gwen tried to fight her own disturbing thoughts, but it wasn't easy. Her nerves were strung tight; she felt all courage crumbling.

"You're all right," he said in a reassuring tone.

With the heat of him warming her, and his hand caressing her, she couldn't keep back the emotional turmoil inside her. She blinked hard against tears, pressing her face against the curve of his neck. "You don't need this," she said, aware he didn't understand that much of her fear was for him not herself.

"And you didn't need that."

It was his voice, soft as a whisper that gave her strength. If he was calm, she could be.

As the wind shifted, it threw pelting rain at them. Lightning flashed, then thunder rumbled. She vaguely heard it. The smell and taste of rain were on him, and her senses were caught up in one thing—one man, and blind need and longing for him.

"Don't think about what happened."

"Don't let me," she pleaded, still trembling.

Lying awake in Jack's bed, while he slept beside her, Gwen listened for the soft tapping of rain at the window. The storm had passed. Or had it just subsided for a while? she wondered, soothed by Jack's soft even breaths in the quiet of his bedroom.

She snuggled closer. Never had she wanted a man so much. Never had she yearned—ached with such intensity—for a man's hands on her.

Turning toward him, she pushed her hands against his shoulders and saw the flicker of desire again in his eyes.

"You're so beautiful."

You are, too, she wanted to say. He was more generous than any man she'd ever known. Generous with his kindness, his caring, his blunt honesty. With his seduction, she thought, sighing, as his hand cupped her breast.

She heard him whisper her name, nothing more. Nothing else would have mattered, for nothing he might have said would change what she was feeling for him.

Gwen wondered if she'd even slept an hour. Oddly, despite the terror of the previous night, a sense of peace filled her. She wandered through his living room and scanned the books, his music. She could live here and be comfortable, she acknowledged. She already felt as if she belonged.

She turned toward the kitchen, wondering how she'd begun to feel so much for someone she'd known such a short time. Trust, she realized. She trusted him with her life. Why had she denied what seemed so obvious to her now? She could trust him with her heart, too.

"Do you plan on making breakfast?"

Gwen swung around and stepped into his arms. "Whatever you want," she said softly, pressing close, wishing for words to tell him how much he'd given her.

"What I want can't be found in the kitchen," he said in an amused voice.

She drew back, smiling. "You have an insatiable appetite."

"For you."

Laughing, she slipped away and opened a cupboard, looking for cups. "Two. You have only two glasses, two plates, two of everything in this kitchen."

Jack leaned back in the kitchen chair, enjoying the sight of her in his robe, in his kitchen. "One for each of us."

She maneuvered around his kitchen with the fluid ease that had initially entranced him. It made him think of how sensually slow she'd moved against him last night. He'd felt the aching passion of his teen years, a longing that had threatened to do him in too quickly. Even now, desire threatened to control him again.

"You are a weird man, Sergeant," she said, as she flung open the refrigerator door.

Running his fingers across his unshaven jaw, he watched her take inventory of the contents.

"Are you a health nut? Vegetable juice. Yogurt. Artificial eggs."

He heard surprise in her voice as she selectively rattled off what she saw.

"It's not a crime."

"But you eat greasy hamburgers."

"So, I have a few weaknesses."

"What else?" she asked, her head still in the refrigerator.

"Beer," he muttered, as she pulled out orange juice. "Honey-roasted peanuts."

She closed the refrigerator door with her hip and walked toward him. "What else?"

Jack reached out and snagged her hand. "Greatlooking redheads."

She tumbled onto his lap, laughing. "I guess a few vices can't hurt."

Murmuring into her hair, he asked, "Do you have any?"

"One it seems." She whispered it as she sought his mouth. "You."

"You may regret skipping breakfast." She snatched her purse from the floor of his car and fished for a note she'd scrawled to herself about the recital.

Glancing away from traffic, he chuckled. "Hardly."

The rain had stopped, and sunshine glared against the windows of the car by the time they reached the dance studio. Flicking off the ignition, he turned to look at her over the rim of mirrored sunglasses. "I hate to dull your mood. But keep a low profile today, okay?"

Gwen wondered if he realized how difficult that would be for her. "Promise," she said.

As she preceded him into the dance studio, she mulled over her options. She was determined to be cautious, but she did have a job to do. While her well-being was his problem, she owed her students all her concentration for the next few hours.

The quick click of footsteps echoing from the hallway caught Gwen's attention just as she was dropping her shoulder bag off at the reception desk.

It was Carrie, a bright red cancan costume draped over her arm. She looked harried, one hour before show time. "We have a problem." Leaning close to Gwen, her tone was low, as if she were concerned someone might overhear. "Mandy isn't feeling well."

Gwen stared down the hallway to where her star pupil stood beside her mother. Bright red spots freckled Mandy's glum face. "Oh, Mandy."

A hand on her shoulder, the girl's mother looked as downtrodden as her daughter. "Chicken pox, I think," she said. "She'd been running a low fever but she felt better this morning so I brought her in early for a final rehearsal before the recital. When she came out of the dressing room, they—" She paused and touched her daughter's face. "They were there."

Gwen offered sympathetic words, knowing how disappointed the little girl must be. Tears welling in her eyes, shoulders slumped, Mandy headed with her mother toward the exit.

"Poor thing." Carrie grabbed a recital program off the reception desk. "You'll have to make an announcement to the audience."

Gwen heard her but her attention was focused elsewhere.

Pinned against a wall, as if bubonic plague had been announced, was Jack. He shook his head slowly, his eyes wide. "I've never had chicken pox."

It seemed incongruous that a man who faced bullets as part of his job would look so alarmed about a childhood disease. "Everyone has had chicken pox," Gwen told him.

He frowned with annoyance. "I haven't."

"You'll be all right," she assured him with the good sense not to crack a smile.

A chaotic mood prevailed the rest of the day. While Carrie handed out recital programs to the arriving throng, Gwen organized students for their dance routines. As people crowded into the auditorium, Gwen hurried to finish one last task before the recital began.

Emerging from her office, she nearly plowed into Jack outside the door. Startled, she jumped, pressing a hand to her chest. "Will you stop this? You nearly scared the wits out of me."

Though she said the words lightly, he continued to frown. "Why did you run in there? What's your problem?"

"One you can handle." Gwen leaned closer, simultaneously brushing a kiss to his cheek and poking a video camera into his midsection. "I need someone to run this for me," she said, rearing back from him.

"I can't do this. I need to watch you."

"I promise you that I'll be right by your side the whole time." Gwen knew his concern was sincere and justified, but she just couldn't imagine anything happening during the recital.

"Dammit, Gwen, is nothing uncomplicated with you?"

She knew he just wanted to keep her safe, but his words shot a sadness through her. She hadn't expected this from him. Her family said similar words constantly.

He grabbed her chin and forced her eyes to meet his. She saw his wry grin, felt the fingers of his other hand brushing hers as they slid around the camera. "I'm going to hold you to that promise," he said.

Instantly she realized how much she'd overreacted to a few simple words. Why had she taken his teasing words so seriously? She had to believe in him, trust him. Hadn't he already proven that he accepted her as she was? "I like you, Sergeant," she murmured against his lips. "A lot."

"I like you, too," he returned lightly. "But you'd better glue yourself to my side or I'll kill you."

Laughing, Gwen danced away from the hand on her chin. Still, as best she could, she planned to keep her word.

Several hours later, Gwen stood at the side of the stage, exuberant with pride. Her youngest dance student, an impish four-year-old, was finishing her rendition of "Singing in the Rain."

Applause echoed off the walls as the performers reappeared for a final round of clapping.

Gwen couldn't stop beaming when one of the students presented her with a bouquet. Flowers cradled in her arms, she wove her way through the crowd of smiling parents to reach her office. Jack followed right behind her. "Weren't they great? They all did so well." Excited, she knew she was rambling. "Did you get all of it on tape?" she asked, as Jack reached around to open her office door.

"Of course. I feared you would curse me with chicken pox if I didn't." His amused tone halted abruptly as he stared into the room.

Glancing in herself, Gwen needed no explanation.

Her hands primly folded on Gwen's desk, Ardelle smiled back stiffly.

## Chapter Eight

To say Gwen was surprised would have been an understatement. "You came?" She stepped closer. "How nice."

"Yes, I came. I came to see how *this* was going," Ardelle said with an elegant backhand motion in no specific direction. "It was mildly successful."

Gwen heard the door click behind her and realized Jack had gone. She wanted to whip around and flee with him. She wished he'd stayed. It was a fleeting cowardly thought. He couldn't protect her from everything, and she wouldn't expect him to. "It was very successful," she corrected her sister, determined to keep her voice steady.

Looking down, Ardelle adjusted the silk cuff on her blouse. "I didn't see any of our friends anywhere."

Gwen knew where Ardelle was headed. In her sister's eyes, success of any gathering was measured by the magnitude of well-known faces and celebrities around her. Gwen's buoyant spirits deflated. One little word of praise, she mused. That was all she had hoped for. She counted to five before meeting her sister's stare head-on. "There is a houseful of nice people out there, Ardelle."

"Really, Gwen." She rolled her eyes melodramatically, then focused on a small, plastic figure of a woman wearing a crown and cape. "You know I had hoped you would realize how ridiculous this whim of yours is."

World's Best Teacher was crudely printed beneath the statue. A present from one of her students, a treasure to Gwen. She resisted the urge to yank if from her sister's hand.

Frowning, Ardelle set down the figure and slowly turned her head to Gwen. "Father has always been too indulgent with you, because he missed you for so many years."

Gwen weathered the wave of guilt she felt at the reminder. "What is this all about?" she asked impatiently.

"A talk that we should have had long before now." Her sister's tone remained dry and clipped. "I feel it is my place to tell you that you have already embarrassed the family enough by opening this plebeian dance studio. You're an Ashcroft," she stated emphatically. "You have certain responsibilities."

"Such as?" Gwen asked, determined to keep her temper under control. "Teas, charities? They're fine for you but not me. I'm not you, Ardelle. I don't care about seeing my name on the newspaper society page.''

Ardelle responded predictably. With the dignity of an offended queen, she said with deliberate slowness, ''You owe your family certain considerations. Closing this studio would be a good start. But there is something else.''

Gwen mentally prepared herself.

''Though your fiancé is pleasant, he's hardly suitable for an Ashcroft.''

''You don't know anything about him.''

''That's correct.'' She rose slowly. ''Ralston is checking on his family.''

''Ah,'' Gwen said with a mirthless laugh. Restless with annoyance, she strolled around her desk and leaned back against a file cabinet. ''I see. This is microscope time.''

''Don't be flippant.''

She didn't want to be, but how else could she protect herself? An old ache was returning. Words not said before were suddenly close to the surface between them.

''I'm sorry,'' Ardelle said so awkwardly that Gwen wondered when she'd last apologized to anyone. ''I don't mean to sound cruel about him. But the truth is obvious. Your fiancé has nothing in common with us. He could make millions, but he is not from the right family.''

''Is that what Father said?'' Gwen asked.

''No. He has his own problems, he's got no time to discuss yours.''

"So you decided to handle what you consider a family crisis?"

A faint flush stained her sister's cheeks. "Someone has to."

Sadness filled Gwen. Staring at the bouquet cradled in her arm, she thought back to the joy she'd felt when she'd received it. Though she viewed life differently than her sister did, somehow she had to reach an understanding with her. "I know you mean well, and hurting any of you is the last thing I want to do, but this studio is important to me." Gwen drew a long breath. "And who I choose may not always please you, but then you don't always please me," Gwen said without anger.

Ardelle squinted, her eyes suddenly moist. Seeing her sister's head bow slightly, Gwen swayed, wanting to go to her. But with one gesture, she froze Gwen to the spot. Stoically, Ardelle straightened her back and raised her head. "Perhaps, it's time Father gets involved." Her voice was heavy with censure once again. "I only hope he will be able to make you act more sensibly."

Gwen didn't want to be sensible. Just happy. I love you, she wanted to tell her sister, watching her storm toward the door. But sometimes I don't like you.

Slouched lazily against the hallway wall, Jack jolted to face Ardelle as the office door swung open. For a moment she paused and stood stiffly before him, her hand gripping the handles of her purse so tightly that her knuckles whitened.

He felt invisible. She wasn't really looking at him, he realized. She was seeing a threat against what she considered sacred.

As she stalked away, the office door opened again.

Jack watched Gwen with cop's eyes, looking for telltale signs of her mood in her body language. Head bent, she hid her face as she shoved a video cassette into the side pocket of her shoulder bag. He wanted to see her eyes, know if the hurt previously in her voice still existed.

"Sorry, I took so long."

As she raised her face to him, he saw sadness but no tears, and in her voice, he heard an underlying strength. A shaft of longing cut through him. More than passion bound him to her. He wanted her to be his, he wanted to protect her from such pain. But he knew instead he might be the cause of it if he didn't back away from her.

"Do you think it's possible some of us might be blood relatives to Attila the Hun?"

He chuckled noncommittally but wondered how a woman as warm and caring and passionate as she was could come from such icy stock. "You should be proud. The recital was great." He opened his arms to her, and she stepped forward into his embrace without hesitation.

"I am."

"So am I," he said to the face raised to him. Despite her strained smile, unhappiness still dulled her eyes. His hands against the small of her back, he drew her tighter, brushing his lips across her cheek. Holding her close, he felt her aching.

He watched her shake her head as if to banish a thought then step back, her chin up, her back straight. He saw again the strong will she possessed that had snagged his interest from their first meeting. She amazed him with her ability to find some brightness through shadows of adversity.

"We have to make one stop first," she said when they reached the car.

Though the man in him would give her anything she wanted, the cop in him considered protesting. But even the cop knew better. She was a stubborn woman. If she wanted to go somewhere, she'd get there.

A gentle breeze whipped around them and blew her hair forward around her face. She tossed her head back, raising a hand to catch her hair. "This tape is for Mandy. I want to drop it off at her house. Okay?"

Jack wasn't surprised. He'd seen her caring nature before. Even when her sister had voiced words so harsh that Jack would have turned his back on her, Gwen had stayed and listened. He'd often sensed her aching to reach out to Ardelle to give her sisterly affection. She gave without hesitation, any way she could, and one small girl would benefit this time.

Before opening the car door for her, he tucked the errant strands of hair behind her ear, wanting by some small measure to do something for her. "Yeah, okay."

"Oh, good." Her frown gave way to a genuine smile, one that warmed him. "Sometimes you're so rigid about my safety. I was afraid you'd refuse. And I really want her to have this," she said, cupping a hand over the top of the tape sticking out of her purse. "I know how important the recital was to her."

"Whatever you want," he said simply. Anything, he thought—everything.

"So was she happy?"

"Thrilled." Gwen stared out the window. With each mile that brought them closer and closer to her father's house, she grew more and more anxious. "Before I left, Mandy was already on the telephone talking to friends about the tape," she added, but her own excitement over the recital was ebbing noticeably.

By the time they passed through the security gate, it was almost five o'clock. Gwen's stomach nervously fluttered. For years, the elegant house had symbolized too many limitations, the intruding media, carefully screened friends. She had thought that by now she'd be free from all that. But here she was again, and once more the freedom was gone.

"God, but I wish we could sneak upstairs," she whispered into Jack's ear as they stood in the foyer.

Late-afternoon sunlight flooded the elegant hallway. As the tall double doors of the living room opened, Gwen saw family members perched on the silk-upholstered sofas and chairs. She had no doubt that they'd been discussing her. She could imagine the words. *Gwen's doing it again, embarrassing the family.* She fought an urge to run. Running hadn't helped her before and it wouldn't now. At the sound of footsteps, she instinctively pressed closer to Jack.

"I thought I heard you," Trish said too brightly, as she emerged from the room. Her back to the others, she gave Gwen a desperate pleading look, as if being held hostage and restrained from yelling for help.

Jack unlaced his fingers from Gwen's. "I have to talk to Earl," he said low. "Be tough. Like you are with me," he teased.

Gwen gave him a reassuring nod. She didn't feel strong, she realized. She felt young and uncertain and inadequate. But one look at Trish forced her to suppress her own self-doubts. Trish needed her, she reminded herself, pushing away the urge to retreat. Forcing a smile, she marched to the rescue, aware her sister was reaching for a lifeline.

"Your recital went well, didn't it?" Trish asked gaily. "I wanted to come but Ardelle had already made appointments for me with several jewelers so I could decide on my bridesmaids' gifts. And she was having a real fit about you not getting home in time for a final gown fitting."

Gwen waited for Trish to take a needed breath. "How did you know about the recital?" she asked, loud enough for the ears perked in the other room to eavesdrop.

In a conspiring whisper, Trish spoke out of the corner of her mouth. "Ardelle's been unbearable since she returned. What happened between you two?" For the benefit of others, she pitched her voice to a shrilly bright tone. "Ardelle told us about it. She said you were pleased." Hooking an arm over Gwen's, Trish tugged her. "Come with me and see the gifts that have arrived."

Gwen allowed herself to be dragged into the adjacent drawing room. Exquisitely wrapped gifts covered the surface of a rosewood sideboard.

"What is happening?" Trish held her arm so tightly that Gwen winced.

"Hey, hey. You're stopping the blood in my arm."

Trish released her death grip. "Sorry. But I thought you'd never get back. It's been terrible here without you."

Gwen heard what wasn't said. *They're ganging up on me.* She inched over to the sideboard and scanned the gifts. "What did Ardelle say when she came home?"

"That you were being your usual self."

Gwen felt hurt, but hid it. Trish needed lightness most of all. "That's reassuring."

The humor reached Trish, easing the tension from her face. "She said Jack was there, and she told Aunt Ursula and Ralston that she tried to reason with you about him, but you were being obstinate."

"Ah, a lynching," Gwen murmured lightly.

"Yes, and Aunt Ursula aided and abetted. She—" As if someone had flicked a switch, Trish stopped suddenly.

"Go on," Gwen urged.

Averting Gwen's eyes, her sister practically squirmed.

"Trish." Gwen said her name firmly to jolt the words out of her.

"She said it's reprehensible for an Ashcroft to consider marrying a man of such common beginnings."

Gwen laughed at the quote. "Good old Auntie."

"Gwen, don't take her so lightly. She is—well..." She paused, worry back in her voice. "Maybe if she was told that he's not really your fiancé, if she knew that you were only pretending, then—"

Gwen raised a halting hand to her. "I don't plan on telling her anything. No one is supposed to know that, so you aren't to say anything. Jack could be the only real protection Father will have during your wedding."

"But couldn't you tell him not to be so convincing? Ardelle claimed that you were acting overly demonstrative and—"

Gwen felt genuine amusement and relief sweeping over her. She couldn't help laughing. "Holding his hand would be overly demonstrative to her."

Trish's frown resurfaced. "Why aren't you taking any of this seriously? You don't have to go through all this criticism. After it's over they'd understand—"

Gwen couldn't help herself. She smiled.

As Trish's eyes rounded, Gwen imagined the wheels turning in her sister's head. "It might not be over between you two. That's why you don't care?" Disbelief edged her voice. "Something *is* going on?"

As Trish gasped, Gwen raised a finger to her lips. "Ssh."

"You and—oh, Gwen," she said, obviously worried. "Gwen, he's—"

"He's not like the others. He's honest. Most of all, I trust him."

"But they won't accept him," Trish said with certainty, inching closer.

Gwen knew she was right, but she couldn't allow herself to think about it. "Would you?"

"Yes, but I'm—"

Gwen placed her hands on her sister's arms. "That's all I wanted to hear," she said softly. Winking, she turned away and rushed up to her room to change for the party.

By eight-thirty that evening, a gigantic diamond sparkled on Gwen's hand. The engagement ring had been an unexpected complication for Jack. He should have thought of it. Hadn't she even slipped him a reminder? He'd replied like a smart ass then, certain he wouldn't like the assignment or the woman he had to guard. Almost overnight he'd changed his mind. Almost overnight he'd become obsessed with her. And now? Now, he was in love with her.

He would have hocked everything he owned, just to buy her the best ring possible. Even so, it would have seemed like a chip in comparison to the rock her father had thrust at him.

Decked out in a tuxedo, Jack stood in the living room of her aunt's Georgian home. His collar tight, he squirmed in discomfort. He was eager to get the evening over with, get out of the monkey suit.

Beside him, Gwen was conversing with a gray-haired man about the cultural differences she'd faced in Morocco.

She looked beautiful in an ice-blue silk dress that bared one shoulder. The clingy material ripened a man's fantasy about what was beneath it. "This isn't my idea of a party," he whispered to her.

Sliding her arm around his back, Gwen leaned closer. "Talk to me later," she teased, feeling eyes watching them. She wanted to tell them all to believe what they saw. For her, the charade was over. The man beside her had done something she'd thought was impossible. He'd made her shed doubts about ever feeling strongly for any man again.

As Jack slipped away, weaving his way toward the white-jacketed servant behind the bar, Gwen nodded politely to comments about Trish and Wesley being a match made in heaven.

Overhead, a rainbow of colors danced in the crystal chandelier, reflecting the peacock finery of the women in the room. Around her, voices buzzed with conversation, ice cubes clicked in glasses, and music drifted through the air. But the party was boring to Gwen, too. She could have told Jack that she'd always felt as out of sync as he did at these gatherings. At the moment, she thought she'd yawn in their face if one more woman mentioned her volunteering for some hospital fund-raiser or charity luncheon.

From across the room, Trish caught her eye and mouthed for her not to move. Looking radiant in a pale peach chiffon gown, she breezed her way past couples to sidle close. "Wait until you hear what's happening now!"

Gwen pulled her arm out from her sister's clamping grip. "What is the matter with you?"

Guiding Gwen out of earshot of the couples entering the room, Trish looked ready to burst with news. "Aunt Ursula is going to announce your engagement publicly tonight."

"She can't."

"She is."

She did.

"When is the wedding?" someone asked, cornering her and Jack near the spiral staircase.

Gwen glanced up at Jack with the loving adoration of a woman bewitched. "We haven't decided yet," she said, a little slower than usual, as Jack's eyes met hers with a soft, affectionate look more disturbing than one filled with desire. "Right now, the family is too busy with Trish's wedding to think about another one."

"Everyone was so surprised," one woman gushed, arching her brow.

Gwen smiled sweetly back at her. She knew she'd be the hot topic of gossip by morning.

Beside her, Jack let out a long breath. He tipped his head toward her, but whatever gibe he'd planned to make was lost when Ardelle sidled close.

"We did handle that well, didn't we? Now, if only someone else would stop acting like a horse's ass," she said.

Gwen traced Ardelle's stare.

"Do you see that?" she asked outraged, eyeing the thin brunette standing beside Wesley. "Riffraff. Who is she?"

Gwen held back an I-told-you-so feeling of satisfaction that Perfect Wesley was revealing a flaw. "The governor's niece."

Ardelle looked a little uncertain for a moment— only a moment—then marched toward the couple.

Watching her sister storm away, Gwen suddenly was struck with weariness from having to make up too many answers. She forced a smile for a silver-haired couple passing by. Jack felt her weight change against him as if she needed support. "You, okay?" he asked softly, sensing the lies were wearing her down.

"I'm fine." She raised her gaze to meet his. "Do you think we're convincing?"

His eyes never left her face, his breath floating across her cheek like the warm flutter of a summer's breeze. Bending closer, he brushed his lips against her jaw. "I think you're beautiful."

His voice caressed her like soft velvet, relaxing her. She smiled up at him. It was the first genuine smile she'd felt all evening, and it was because of him. Suddenly her impatience to leave was unbearable. She glanced around the room, as if looking for an escape route.

And then she saw the cello case. In an adjacent room where the help was setting up chairs for guests, it stood upright in a corner. Nothing had prepared her. She knew instantly she couldn't handle this last development in an evening that already seemed too long. Even before the slim, dark-haired man who'd just entered the room turned around, she knew she'd be facing Justin.

Mentally Jack prepared himself for some highbrow music. If the cellist didn't perform "Brahms Lullaby," he wouldn't know what was being played. He preferred rock music. Sitting at a stakeout after midnight, he needed wailing electric guitars to keep him alert. He knew more about Bon Jovi than Wagner. Another reason to want the evening over. Surrounded by brocade furniture, heavy gold drapes, and gilt-framed Renoirs, he didn't belong here, he thought. He would never fit in.

Glancing at the french doors, he yearned to step outside and breathe in the wood-scented air, instead of the sweet staleness around him from too many perfumes and too many flowers.

He scanned the sea of faces for John Austin Ashcroft, saw him conversing with some man Jack had been introduced to. Detective Lyndon, Ashcroft's so-called new assistant, stood at his side, appearing to be glued to his employer as if his success might rub off on him.

Appearances didn't matter to Jack or Lyndon. What other people thought about them wasn't important. They were there to do a job. Protecting the Ashcrofts wasn't an easy task. People filled the room. People who claimed ancestors from the Mayflower or the American Revolution. Worlds apart, he thought again, glancing at Gwen. She shifted beside him, seeming restless.

As she drew away slightly, he curled a hand around her shoulder. Conversation lowered to a hum as the cellist crossed the room. He looked soft to Jack. A thin, handsome, dark-haired man, a pampered man with hands as delicate as a woman's.

Jack felt an unmistakable tenseness in Gwen's body. The small of her back seemed to draw forward in some protective instinct. With just one glance, he knew something was wrong. Vulnerability contorted her face seconds before she whipped around as if suddenly being chased.

As she wove a path around guests, he followed quickly, never losing sight of her. He was only two steps behind her when her older sister and a gray-haired man blocked his way. Eyes glued to Gwen's back, Jack nodded and shook the man's hand. With a quick excuse, he sidestepped them, desire to protect Gwen rising within him.

He found her standing near an ivy trellis, bathed in the moonlight slanting across the lush grass. "Can we escape together?" he asked, unsure of her mood.

"I need to be alone."

"No dice," he said firmly, stepping out of the shadows.

Pale, she shivered and hugged herself though the air was warm. "I don't want company."

Because she sounded so close to tears, he deliberately chose tougher words. "I don't give a damn. You can't be alone."

"Of course not. What I want isn't important. It never is." Her voice trailed off, her eyes blinking as if she couldn't see clearly. "I'm sorry. You didn't deserve that."

"It's okay," he soothed. He sensed he shouldn't rush her, and set a palm against the trellis close to her shoulder. "Do you want to tell me what happened in there?"

"An old lover showed up," she admitted in a tone that was weighed down with disgust. "No one will question that I left. We had a bitter breakup, quite loud and very public. So everyone knows that I was engaged to a man who cared more about my being a member of the Ashcroft family than being with the woman he loved." As though she'd been running too fast, she drew a hard breath. "Jack, I really want to be alone."

"You know I can't do that."

"Oh, God, I hate this." She offered him her back again. "When will we be able to move around without looking over our shoulders, without someone shadowing us?"

At the hurt in her voice, Jack curled his fingers over her shoulders. "Let me help."

"I made a fool of myself for the second time."

Her body went soft against him. Her total helplessness stunned him. She was a fighter, someone who willingly battled if she felt trapped. Lightly he touched her hair, smoothed it, then turned her in his arms to face him. "You're allowed three shots at that."

"Are you?" she asked, not sounding convinced.

"Sure." He wanted to comfort her, see the smile he'd begun to look forward to. "Does he mean that much to you?"

Her eyes locked with his. "How can you ask that? I wouldn't have been with you, if he did."

He heard hurt in her voice and damned himself for letting his own misgivings about them surface when she needed him.

"He doesn't mean anything to me anymore except a bruised pride. But I can't shake the old ache. He wanted something from me," she said softly, indicating it was difficult to admit. "I was the means to the end. Money has a curse to bear. You never know when someone really cares for you. When I met him, everyone was thrilled and sighed with relief. I can't blame them. I came close to marriage a few times. But they were all the wrong kind."

"Did you think they were wrong?"

Confusion knitted her brows. "Did I... That is what counts, isn't it?" She didn't wait for his response. "I've tried so hard to fit in during the past few years, to be a part of the family again. At least I thought I had." She shook her head to push away a thought. "But looking back, I could say now that I knew the men I'd chosen were wrong for me."

Her words weren't easy for him to hear. He wondered if she'd have the same thoughts about himself eventually.

"One was a Czechoslovakian acrobat. I met him at a circus while I was in Germany. He wasn't exactly befitting of an Ashcroft." As her voice softened, he leaned closer, straining to hear her words. "I was young, nineteen and easily enchanted by the dark, handsome types. I became less impressed with him quickly. He wanted American citizenship the easy way—via marriage. Another of my poor choices was a championship rodeo bull rider. He wanted to be introduced to a New York television producer and become the next Wheaties man. Neither one pleased my family."

"And then there was the cellist," Jack said in a questioning tone.

"Yes and then there was the cellist. A dignified proper man with all the right credentials to satisfy the family. But he, too, had ulterior motives." She spit out the last words as if they'd stung her tongue. "I believed he loved me. Everyone was so pleased that I'd found someone suitable, and so I fooled myself."

"Everyone does at some time," he reminded her.

"Yes, I suppose they do. But I wasn't prepared. I was looking for honest feelings. Those other men were only interested in what I could do for them. When Justin came along, I thought he was different. He was the grandson of a renowned Metropolitan Opera star. He'd studied at Julliard. I didn't think he would want anything from me but me." Her voice wavered, and she blinked hard against the tears welling in her eyes.

He didn't want to hear about this man, about any man in her life. "Don't waste those on him," he said, drawing her close.

"They're for me, not him," she said softly. Gwen wasn't sure why she was crying, except too many dreams had been lost too often to lies.

"Why were you attracted to him?"

She brought forth a faint smile. "I thought he was nice at one time."

He looked puzzled. "A hell of a reason."

She didn't think so. She was with Jack for that reason. Because beneath the toughness, she'd discovered a nice man. "What reason is better?" she asked.

With a touch so light she barely felt it, he brushed a knuckle across her cheek. "You shouldn't have to ask. Sparks," he whispered.

She breathed deeply, the clean, masculine scent of him filling her mind.

"Heat," he said huskily, his mouth hovering close to hers.

Yes, heat, she mused. She wanted that, too, and suddenly considered herself lucky to have found so much in one man.

As his palms framed her cheeks and he lowered his mouth to hers, she heard sounds of the party, but she was caught up in her own celebration, in her own fireworks, her own excitement. With his caress, she felt more than desire, more than compassion. He cared about her, she realized. He truly cared about her.

When they reentered the room, Gwen braved Justin's stares as he approached. Politely she smiled at him, but she kept her hand tightly linked with Jack's.

He felt her squeezing, as if drawing strength from him to get through the difficult moment. He didn't doubt Gwen's words that she had no feelings for the man anymore, but that didn't make the moment easier.

Bennett smiled at her and, in cultured tones, carried on inconsequential conversation about his latest trip to Europe. Even if this was the wrong man for her, he wasn't the wrong type. Jack wanted to slug the bastard for hurting Gwen, and for reminding him of how different his life-style was from hers.

His anger hadn't completely abated when he and Gwen returned to the house. He paced in his room for nearly half an hour before giving in to what he needed most to soothe him. "Everyone is sleeping," he said, when Gwen opened her bedroom door to him seconds later.

"Good, because I've decided you work too hard."
She draped a hand over his shoulder and leaned forward to scan the hallway. "And I have a remedy."

Despite the shadowed light, he could see the sparkle in her eyes and feel the tension from his own thoughts slipping away. "Is it relaxing?"

"Not too," she said, looking down and unbuttoning his shirt.

Staring at the crown of her head, he inhaled deeply, wondering if her sweet scent would haunt him years from now. An arm at her waist, he tugged her closer until her soft contours felt as one with him. Then he backed her up slowly into the room. With a kick, he closed the door behind him. "I need you," he groaned fiercely, not allowing himself to say the words of love that ached for release.

## Chapter Nine

Gwen awoke slowly, dreams and reality mingling. Peeking out of one eye, she stared at the window and saw a hint of rose streaking across the sky. A storm coming? she wondered, shifting to curl closer to Jack. But the strong, hard body that had warmed her during the night wasn't there.

She jerked up her head, wanting to see him, needing the reassurance that the time with him hadn't been part of a dream. Leaning on an elbow, she saw him standing at the far wall of her bedroom. She dropped back to the pillow reassuredly, squirming to the spot on the sheet where his warmth still lingered.

"Hey, lazy. This yours?"

Reluctantly she pushed herself up and jammed a pillow behind her back to see what he was referring to.

He was pointing at her scrawled signature in the corner of a painting of a stormy-gray, ominous sky and crashing waves beating at a sailboat.

With his warm gaze on her, self-consciously she combed through tousled strands of her hair. "It's not Picasso's."

"It's good. Would you sell it?"

She was stunned by his question. "You want it?"

Grinning in a way that she was becoming familiar with, he reached for his belt from the top of her dresser. "How much?" he asked, slipping it through the loops in his jeans.

She was slow to respond. "I don't know."

"Think about it. I'd like it for my living room."

Pleasure from his words rocketed through her. She'd been prepared for some polite pleasantries about her painting being nice. She'd expected him to shrug noncommittally, because he truthfully hated it but politeness prevented criticism.

"What price?" he asked again, strolling toward her.

"No price," she said with finality. She wanted to linger in bed, indulge herself, pull him back down to her. But when he grabbed her robe from the foot of the bed and held it out for her, she sighed and wiggled out from between the sheets.

The moment she slid her arms into the robe, his embrace wrapped around her, his palm splayed her belly. Feather-light, his tongue traced a slow path around the shell of her ear. "Name a price." His mouth taunted her ear a moment longer before he turned her into his arms. "Don't you want anything from me?'' he murmured against the curve of her neck.

Sparked by the humor in his eyes, she gave him a playful reply. "I thought you might want something from me."

"Only what you want to give me."

Raw emotion overwhelmed her. His words were far more special than he'd ever realize. No one had ever made that offer to her before. Almost desperately she wanted to believe those words, believe in him. And love? Maybe, just maybe, she could believe in it, too.

"Think about it." He skimmed her thigh before reluctantly drawing back. "I have to go. Let's see if I can sneak out of here as easily as I sneaked in last night."

Gwen linked her hand with his. "I'll walk with you to the door." As he reached for the doorknob, he swung back to her. She saw questions in his eyes. Did he need constant confirmation, too, that this was real between them? At the moment she had but one thought—ease the worry from his mind. Straightening her shoulders, she held out her hand for a handshake. "See you tonight, Sergeant."

As she'd hoped, he released a quick, astonished laugh at her feigned formality. His hand closed over hers tightly as he brought it to his lips to kiss her palm. "You were enchanting, Ms. Ashcroft."

She arched a brow. "Truly talented?"

"Exceptional."

When the door closed behind him, Gwen eyed the bed longingly. Before she gave in to the urge to jump back in, she forced herself to wiggle into her jeans. She thought nothing could dampen her good mood, until she opened her bedroom door and stepped into the hallway. From downstairs, she could hear her father's agitated voice.

"You're supposed to be guarding my daughter. So where the devil were you earlier this morning? I sent Horton to your room and you weren't there."

She didn't need to see Jack to know he was the one her father was bellowing at. She hurried down the steps.

In the foyer, his back to her, Jack stood rigid, tense. She wasted no time. A rush of color brightened her father's cheeks, warning of his rising anger. "Father." She caught his attention and his frown. "Father, calm down," she said soothingly. She touched his arm, deliberately avoiding Jack's stare. "You'll be waking up the whole house." Hearing the clamor of more footsteps on the staircase, Gwen knew she had only a few seconds. "Really, I was all right," she said softly.

"You don't have to worry," Jack added just as quietly. "I won't let anything happen to your daughter."

"What is going on?" Ralston insisted. His intrusion saved Gwen for the moment from the uncomfortable explanation she sensed her father would insist on.

Lagging behind him, her hair tousled, Trish yawned. "Who's yelling?"

A few steps behind her trailed Ardelle. Her hair was in such perfect order, Gwen had to wonder if she'd slept in a chair.

"Everything is all right," her father said, in a voice meant to end the questions. Snapping a sharp shrewd look briefly at Jack, he continued, "Jack and I had a disagreement about something minor."

Though he forced a slight smile, Gwen noted the tension in Jack's face. She'd told him that her family didn't matter, but she had to face the truth. After years of being at odds with her family, she still longed for their approval.

Mumbling some excuse, Jack disappeared outside. Gwen wanted to follow but, feeling her sister's critical stare, she strolled into the dining room for breakfast.

Standing at the buffet table, Gwen listened to Ardelle complain about Trish's lack of cooperation. Ralston had apparently been hounding Trish to attend some quasi-business function with Wesley tomorrow evening. Trish had been doing her best to stand by her refusal.

"She has certain duties to perform," Ardelle pointed out. "If she wants to be a good wife to Wesley, she'd better accept them."

Beside Gwen, Ralston agreed while piling scrambled eggs on a plate. "So true." He lifted the lid of a silver dish and revealed a bowl of fruit compote to Gwen. "Ardelle and I have decided that your father is acting peculiar."

"Yes," Ardelle added from her seat at the table. "We don't believe for a moment that he was having some minor disagreement with *your* fiancé. Father was shouting." Cradling her coffee cup, Ardelle sent her an expectant look. "What was he so angry about?"

Gwen shrugged dumbly. "The World Series."

"Your father doesn't like baseball," Ralston said in his usual upbraiding tone.

"And where is your fiancé now?" Ardelle demanded. "And Trish?" she added, sounding unnaturally confused. "She's acting strange, too."

Gwen offered a palms-up gesture in response. "Somewhere. But she has good reason to be miserable."

"I am not interested in arguing with you again," Ardelle said stiffly. "Only *you* believe that she's making a mistake. Everyone else thinks Wesley is perfect for her."

"Everyone else isn't Trish. She—" Gwen cut her words short as Earl barreled into the room from the kitchen. His dark eyes darted from Gwen to Ralston to Ardelle and then back to Gwen.

True to form, Ralston exploded. "What are you doing in here!"

Earl frowned in puzzlement and looked to Gwen as if needing a rescuer.

Seeing him shoot a worried look toward the foyer, Gwen could only guess that he'd come in because he couldn't find Jack and urgently needed to talk to him. "Are you supposed to drive Trish somewhere?" she asked, to give him an excuse for barging into the family quarters.

"Yes, ma'am."

"Well, you had better wait in the kitchen."

"Yes, ma'am. Thank you, ma'am," he said, backing out of the room.

Ardelle heaved a heavy breath. "He is absolutely impossible. The man has no experience. He doesn't even know his place. Why in the world did Father hire *him?*"

Gwen set down her empty plate. "Trish needed a chauffeur. Father was probably under pressure to find one quickly."

"He never hired a chauffeur just for me before I got married."

Detecting a hint of sibling rivalry, Gwen wanted to laugh. "Ardelle, you're so efficient," she said, inching her way toward the archway. "He probably didn't think you needed his help. But you know how Trish is. She's never organized."

"Yes, that is true," she replied, sounding pleased.

Gwen flashed a smile at her, then sprinted toward the stairs. Within seconds, she was rushing back down the stairs and out the door. Her heart leaped when she saw several detectives gathered near the gardener's shed. Something was seriously wrong. She didn't want to think about another bomb threat. As Earl rushed around the side of the house, Gwen ran to him. "I couldn't find Jack."

"I found him," he answered. Seeming distracted, he looked away.

Gwen grabbed his arm. "What's going on?"

He fidgeted uncomfortably. "I can't find your sister. I was supposed to drive her to a friend's home at eight o'clock. She never mentioned changing her plans."

"She must be in the house."

"No, she isn't. Horton checked. We can't find her. Hillary said she had a cup of coffee in the kitchen, glanced at the clock, then hurried out the back door." He looked confused. "But no one has seen her since then."

"Where's Jack?"

"He's talking to the men at the gate."

Gwen watched him scurry away to join the other detectives. Frowning, she stared at the woods behind the house. When Trish was younger, if troubled, she always went to the pond on the other side of the estate.

On a hunch, Gwen ran down the path toward the pond. As the shimmer of blue between the trees came into view, she felt discouraged not to see her sister on the grass near it. Where could she be? What if—Gwen banished the thought as she felt her heart skip. Nothing has happened, she berated herself.

At a loss for where else to look for her, she started to retrace her path back to the house. She took only a few steps.

"What are you doing here?" Jack called out, striding toward her.

Gwen interpreted his mood as worried annoyance, not anger. "Looking for my sister. Earl said—" Her voice trailed off as she saw him look past her. Whipping around, Gwen saw her sister emerging from behind bushes off of the trail. Head bent, for a few seconds she wasn't even aware of them watching her.

Suddenly realizing they were there, she stopped and reared back defensively. Her brow wrinkled in confusion and worry. "Is something wrong?"

"You're what's wrong," Gwen yelled, as relief to see her sister safe mingled with irritation. "Why don't you tell people where you're going? Everyone is out looking for you."

"I'm sorry." Trish glanced at Jack to extend the apology to him.

Squinting against the sunlight, Gwen made out movement behind her sister. Jack brushed her hip with his and stepped in front of her, but not before Gwen recognized Fred and the security guard. Glancing at Trish, Gwen saw her sister ready to crumble.

Backing up as if Fred carried some communicable disease, she hunched her shoulders in a protective manner. "I don't want to see you." She shook visibly, tears gathering in her eyes, as she yelled, "I never want to see you again."

"Trish," Fred wailed.

"Never," she added with theatrical flare, before storming back toward the house.

Gwen met Jack's gaze and rolled her eyes. "I'd better talk to her." Because Fred looked so discouraged, she first reassuringly touched his arm. "She's confused. She loves you."

Dejection colored his voice. "She hates me."

Gwen sighed at the idiocy of the moment.

Discreetly Jack signaled the detective to leave.

Standing with his shoulders stooped, Fred cursed. "She hates me."

Amusement lightened Jack's irritation. "Look, you can't wander in here whenever you feel like it. There is a front gate."

"You don't know what these people are like," Fred agonized.

Jack could have told him differently but remained silent.

"I can't get in. Her father won't let me see her."

Jack couldn't believe that this kid, obsessed by love, could be involved with someone like Farrow. But neither could he take the chance of telling him that it wasn't Ashcroft, but police security, that was blocking him from trying to get Trish to talk to him.

"I'll get her to listen to me. I'll do something to make her listen."

Jack offered a warning. "Don't do anything dumb."

"I love her," he said hotly.

"Don't let that love make you do anything foolish." As Fred shrugged and pivoted away, Jack's own words lingered. Why didn't he listen to his own advice? he wondered.

Gwen raced back to the house. She imagined that Jack wasn't in the best mood at the moment. Neither was she. Her sister wasn't being reasonable.

Minutes later, influenced by thoughts of hammering some sense into her, Gwen rapped louder than necessary on Trish's door.

Sounding like a disgruntled teenager, Trish yelled, "Leave me alone."

Disgusted over the sobs she heard, Gwen planted her feet and rapped again. Her sister was acting like an idiot. Gwen had little idea how to prevent a catastrophe. "Trish," she appealed, "unlock the door."

Opening the door only a crack, her sister peered out at her.

Gwen braced a foot against the bottom of the door. "Let me in," she insisted.

Trish sniffed hard, her eyes darting in both directions. "You're alone?"

Determined, Gwen nudged against the door with her shoulder. "I'm alone."

Her sister's nose rivaled Rudolph's. Dabbing a tissue at it, she plopped on the bed, looking like a petulant child.

Gwen closed the door behind her and stepped around the bridal veil that Trish had obviously thrown on the floor in a fit of temper. "Tell me what happened."

"Fred won't leave me alone."

Frowning, Gwen bent over to retrieve the veil. "Should he?" Suspicions growing, she asked bluntly, "Why did you go to the pond?"

"I shouldn't have," she said, sniffing hard. "I shouldn't have taken his telephone call or agreed to meet him," she said without a breath.

Gwen snapped to a stand.

"When all of you showed up, I realized there were other people to think about, and I—" She paused, looking down and twisting the tissue in her hands. "I changed my mind."

Gwen shot a look of disbelief at her. "So you ran off, refusing to talk to him?" Gwen dropped the bridal veil to the vanity chair, hoping to suppress her annoyance. With admirable composure, she asked, "How could you do that to him?"

Trish raised a tear-streaked face to her—her moist, blue eyes widening.

"He expected to talk to you. If you really ever loved him, you wouldn't hurt him that way. Why don't you start being honest with yourself and him?"

"He hurt me," she defended and set her lips in a pout.

"How?" Gwen insisted. "Tell me now exactly what he did to you."

As she sniffed and sobbed her way through the details, Gwen listened intently, reading between the lines. By the time Trish had finished her ragged monologue, Gwen was convinced something sneaky had happened. "I don't like the sound of this," she said honestly.

Trish raised a puzzled look. "What do you mean?"

"Something isn't right. You and Fred—" Gwen's words were cut short by a loud hammering at the door.

"Trisha, I need to speak to you," Ardelle demanded.

"Oh, no," Trish murmured, looking beseechingly at Gwen for help.

Before Gwen could reach the door, Ardelle pushed it open. She charged forward, dumped a small bag from Tiffany's on the settee by the window and began to unpack it. "The gifts for your bridesmaids just arrived. The jewelry store failed to send one of them. And I just finished talking to Levan. His allergies are acting up, but he'll be here tomorrow for the final fitting of the gowns."

Glancing back at Gwen, she saw her shrug. "Show some concern," she berated, placing Gwen under heavy scrutiny. "I don't suppose you'll have time to help Trish pack tomorrow for her honeymoon."

At Trish's sniffle, Gwen reached for the tissue box. "Oh, are they going on one?"

Rearing back, Ardelle scowled. "Of course they are. They're going to the Bahamas." She cast a look at Trish. "And what are you crying about?"

"Nothing." Trish sniffled again and snatched up the tissue Gwen had dropped in her lap.

Ardelle sighed. "If anyone saw you, they would think you were unhappy. Such silliness," she murmured. "Now, you do have some real difficulties to deal with. Uncle Carlton will have to be placed in the west wing when he arrives tomorrow evening."

Trish dabbed at her eyes with the tissue. "Why? He's always stayed in the east wing."

"Aunt Sybil will be there." Displeasure seeped into her voice again. "I don't understand either of you," she said, as if they were dim-witted. "He'll be arriving with his second wife. They certainly can't be quartered on the same side of the house as Aunt Sybil."

"It's his third wife, Ardelle," Gwen reminded her.

"Second, third. What difference does it make?"

"Someday they'll say that about you," she mumbled to Trish.

Trish released what sounded like a whimper. "This wedding is going to be a disaster."

Irritation at her younger sister's behavior overwhelmed Gwen. "It might be if you don't get a different groom." As Ardelle opened her mouth, Gwen raised a silencing hand. "I'm leaving."

Ardelle slipped in the reminder just before Gwen walked out the door. "Aunt Ursula will be here for lunch."

Gwen spent the morning curled on a chair in her father's library. At home she would have scrubbed floors to wear off her exasperation, but for her to clean anything in her father's house would have been frowned upon.

Hours later she tossed aside the fifth book she'd tried to concentrate on. Still fuming, she dashed up the stairs to her own room. Where was Trish's gumption? she wondered for the umpteenth time. She'd always been a gentle soul, but she'd also always had a flair for mischief. She'd been as bold and as much her own person as Gwen had been. How, in only a few months, had the vivacious young girl she'd left become such a dull acquiescent lump?

Flinging open the door, she doubted anything would soothe her.

She was wrong.

A second later, she felt as malleable as a marshmallow. Panache, she mused. Jack Mallory had panache. Her heart jumped as she lifted the flower from her pillow. Beneath the blue forget-me-not, he'd left a note: "Sneak out to the pond."

Five minutes later she reached the pond, feeling like an over eager teenager. Winded from her dash through the woods, she slowed down and eyed Jack sprawled out on a blanket, his back against a tree. "Were you looking for me?"

"Always," he said amiably.

When she plopped down beside him, he set the small picnic basket between them. Curious, she reached forward and flipped open the basket. "Thank you for the flower."

He cupped the base of her neck and massaged it lightly. "The gardener will never miss it." Grinning, he inclined his head to see her face as she peered inside the basket.

She lifted out each of the wineglasses, wondering how he could deny a romantic nature. He was the man who left a flower on her pillow and who had a book of poems by Browning in his apartment. "This is nice, but why?"

"We needed time away from the mausoleum," he said, touching her chin and forcing her to look up at him.

She stared into intense pale eyes and remembered the gentleness of his touch lingering on her body. "Do you think anyone will miss us?"

"Lovers are expected to disappear." Deep lines crinkled from the corners of his eyes as he drew away and concentrated on opening a bottle of wine.

Lovers, Gwen mused. Yes, they were, but were they more than that? Refusing to spoil the moment, she fought a flutter of uneasiness that he'd never said love to her. Her effort proved successful. A laugh tickled her throat as she stared at the bundle wrapped in grease-spotted paper. With a deep breath, she inhaled the spicy aroma of chili. "Chili burgers?" At his widening grin, she laughed openly. "Where did you get chili burgers?"

He handed her one. "There's a greasy spoon nearby."

She unwrapped it quickly and took a bite. "You're a godsend," she mumbled. "You saved me from a lunch of lobster bisque. And, while delicious, that wonderful meal includes my aunt's conversation. She's coming to inspect the troops and the barracks."

Regarding her over the rim of his glass, Jack clucked his tongue. "You have no respect."

"Sure I do. But I think after nearly forty years of working here, Hillary doesn't need inspections. She and Horton are loyal employees who would slit their wrists before they'd bring the shame of dusty piano keys to the Ashcrofts."

"What was the backlash of this morning's outburst by your father?" he asked curiously.

"Everyone is mildly confused," Gwen mumbled. "A dilemma for them." With her tongue, she swiped at the sauce on her top lip.

She always amazed him, he realized. He'd seen her elegant in a gown that was probably the equivalent of one of his weekly paychecks. He'd seen her in a sweatshirt and jeans, munching on a chili burger as if it offered the same exquisite rich taste as lobster. "I had no defense to offer your father," he said, handing her a napkin.

Gwen stopped chewing and stared questioningly at him. "You didn't need any."

"He has a right to be worried about your safety. But I couldn't tell him I was loving his daughter all night."

She grinned impishly at the sight of his untouched burger. "That might have been interesting."

"Not funny." His reply came out muffled as he leaned away to set first his wineglass and then hers to the edge of the blanket. Food wasn't on his mind, she decided. "All in all I haven't made things easier for you with your family."

"You haven't done anything wrong."

"Except make trouble for you."

Gwen moved the picnic basket to the grass. "Yes, as you are doing now," she teased. "If you weren't, you'd stop talking and kiss me."

Braced on one palm, Jack leaned closer. "That's sure to lead you into more trouble."

"Trouble?" She tightened her arms around his neck and pulled him down with her. "Who's worried about a little trouble? Not me. Are you?"

"You talk too much," he said, pinning her to the blanket a second before his mouth covered hers and silenced her giggle.

## Chapter Ten

"We need to discuss the wedding, Gwen." Ardelle snagged her arm before she could disappear with Jack after dinner.

"See you later," he whispered against her ear.

Gwen hoped later wouldn't mean hours from now. Surrounded by her sisters and her aunt, she dutifully listened to the last-minute wedding plans. Ardelle took center stage, offering instructions to Gwen and Trish, glancing periodically at her aunt for the matriarch's approval. Moments like this were commonplace.

Gwen had endured enough of them while growing up, and they weren't any easier to tolerate now. Those were the moments she'd wished her father had stepped forward, had been there to rescue them. But he'd been too busy. She couldn't accuse him of neglect. He'd

provided well. He had tried to offer love and understanding, but he'd also convinced himself that raising
daughters was something beyond his expertise. So
Aunt Ursula had a free hand, a heavy one by Gwen's
way of thinking.

By nine-thirty, Gwen was grateful to see her aunt's
eyelids drooping. She felt just as weary herself. Certain she'd fulfilled her responsibility, she excused herself. Climbing the stairs, she wondered where Jack had
disappeared to. She told herself it was asinine to expect him to be in her room waiting for her.

But opening the door, she saw him slouched in a
chair with a book in his hand. Desperately she wanted
to ask, will you always be near? But fear stopped her
from asking the one question that might take him
from her. "What did you do this evening while I was
receiving my instructions?"

He set the book on the table beside him. "Played
poker with Earl and Lyndon."

"Did you win?"

As she crossed to him, he grinned. "I told you.
When I play, I always play to win."

Gwen stood in her bedroom wearing a silly grin.
Leaning back against the door, she touched a finger to
her lips. They still carried the warmth of his. The
quick kiss he'd given her seconds ago before leaving
had held a promise. Of love? she wondered.

Shaking her head quickly, she shied away from the
question, uneasy about challenging what they were
sharing. He'd never said the words because he wasn't

a man who offered words easily, she reasoned. She needed to believe in them—to trust him.

She passed the morning catching up on letters she'd received from friends since her return. When the clock neared noon, she left her room, determined to talk to Trish again. Carrying a cup of coffee, Gwen strolled into the living room with the hope of finding her younger sister.

She found both her sisters.

Ardelle paused in scanning the elegantly wrapped presents just delivered. "Good. You're finally up. Now Trish and I won't have to handle all the last-minute problems alone."

A shoulder braced against a sturdy oak tree, Jack bent his head and lighted a cigarette. To his orderly mind, the occupants in the house bordered on screwy. They were a family that played games with one another. That wasn't his idea of how a family should act, but then he wasn't much of an authority on family life in elite suburbia, or anywhere else for that matter. Blowing out a stream of smoke, he watched as Earl hurried toward him.

"Been looking for you," he said, still a few feet away. "We had trouble last night." He curled a hand around a gnarled oak branch and pivoted toward the security gates. "About midnight, one of our guys saw someone sneaking around the garage."

"Fred Gladstone struck again?"

Earl rocked back on his heels. "I don't know. Before our guy could get to him, he'd jumped over the wall."

"Did you check the garage?"

"And most of the cars but—"

Jack knew the words left unsaid. The possibility existed that a bomb had been planted. Raising a hand, he shielded his eyes from the sunlight to see the name on the delivery truck coming up the driveway toward the house. "When did the wedding gifts begin arriving?"

"A few days ago. But only a few came until this morning."

"Are they giving all of them clearance at the gate?"

Earl tilted his head questioningly. "No. Only store trucks where the bride registered can come in. Like you said, I called the stores and insisted on one specific driver. We've done a security check on them. Why do you ask?"

Jack dropped his cigarette and ground it out. "Who's doing a security check on the gifts?"

Earl's head snapped toward him. "A check on the gifts?" He swore softly.

Jack was already striding away toward the house.

Gwen mentally measured the distance to the archway, wondering if she could make a dash for it.

At the moment, Ardelle's attention focused on Trish. "Levan will be here soon for the final fitting on our dresses."

Gwen made a face, recalling her last meeting with the obnoxious man who lashed his tape measure about like Indiana Jones wielded his whip. "I thought you didn't like his designs, Trish."

"She does," Ardelle insisted.

And that was that, Gwen mused, watching Trish sink to the sofa with a present. Any spark of independence that flared within Trish could be snuffed out instantly by Ardelle's iron fist.

"Are these original creations?" Gwen asked, praying they weren't.

Ardelle glided closer, eyeing the recently delivered presents. "But, of course. Now about what we discussed earlier."

Again? Tension coiled around Gwen like a tight spring. She lifted a present and weighed it in her hands. Another sterling silver bowl? No, a clock, she guessed, by the ticking. Time was passing swiftly for Trish, too. If she didn't wake up soon, she'd find herself married to a jerk like Ralston.

A torturous silence passed as Ardelle skimmed her fingers across several of the unopened packages on the sofa. "Ralston is having a problem securing information about your fiancé's family."

Gwen readied herself for the inquisition. "Probably because Jack has no family."

Fingering the card under a present, Ardelle looked up with a quickness that should have given her whiplash. For a second, her jaw sagged open. "Surely, there must be someone," she said, recovering quickly.

"No one."

Ardelle frowned deeply, but, in a calculating manner that had always made Gwen edgy, she feigned indifference and said nothing else.

As she slipped a card from beneath a white ribbon, Gwen thought of their poor father. She didn't envy him. Soon he was going to be trapped in a long discussion about how unsuitable Jack was.

Bending her head to read the card she'd been fingering, Ardelle breezed on to the next subject in a manner that meant she'd had her say; subject closed. "When I was at Bunny's house, I saw Justin. He spoke to me in private. He's missed you, Gwen."

Not this, Gwen mused. She hadn't expected this kind of attack to weaken her. There's another man in my life, she wanted to yell. A good man. An honest man.

Seeming content to let Gwen mull that announcement over in her mind, Ardelle switched tactics and honed in on Trish. "Trish, you really should have hired him for your wedding. Violins and harps," Ardelle added, raising her chin as if music were floating overhead. "They're lovely. But a cello would expand the repertoire so much." She let the card in her hand flutter to the package and keyed in on Gwen again. "And he does still play beautifully, doesn't he?"

Enough, Gwen decided. She would never accept a clone of Ralston or Wesley. Hadn't she come frighteningly close already when she'd been taken in by Justin? She perched on the arm of the sofa for support before responding. "Ardelle, you have the sensitivity of an armadillo."

"Oh, for goodness' sake," her sister shot back. "Don't be so naive."

"He played me for a fool."

"He did nothing of the sort. I don't know why you were so upset with him. Everyone wants something from someone."

Gwen stared at her thoughtfully, searching for the loving sister she'd known years ago. "Do you seriously believe that?"

"Of course. I'm Ralston's wife. I have what I wanted. And he has the perfect hostess. It's a fact of life, Gwen. We all use each other."

Gwen refused to believe that. She pushed to her feet, not wanting to listen to this stranger any longer.

"Where are you going? You can't leave."

Gwen froze, half-standing, and drew a hard breath. "Why not?"

Ardelle shook her head in a worrisome manner. "I can't understand you. You always want to disappear at the most inappropriate moments."

Realizing she still held one of Trish's wedding presents, Gwen bent forward to set it down. "And this is one of them?"

"Of course it is. What would I say to Levan if you weren't here for the final fitting? I told you he was coming today. When you agreed to Trish's request that you would be in the wedding party, she gave your dress size and measurements to Levan. But a final fitting is absolutely imperative."

She crossed to Gwen and took the package from her hands, seeming to find it more fascinating than any of the others. "Who is this from?" The question wasn't meant to be answered, as with a manicured pink nail, Ardelle flicked the envelope open. "The Farnsworths," she read. "Elise Farnsworth has atrocious taste." She raised the package to her ear. "It ticks," she said with disgust. "Another clock. That woman has a fetish for clocks. If she didn't buy it from some obscure little store, you might be able to return it, Trish."

The frown Gwen had meant for her sister never materialized, as she heard footsteps. Jack stood in the archway, beckoning to her with his head. Who said Rambo wasn't real? Gwen mused, bounding up and rushing to him. "Darling, did you still want to see the horses at the Hentfords?" she asked as an excuse to escape.

Her rescuer proved overeager. He dragged her against him. As she tumbled into his arms, his hands firm at her waist, her body pressed close to his in what had to look like an intimate embrace, Gwen wondered if he would break her windpipe. She placed a hand at his chest to push away from him but froze with his whispered words.

"Don't let her open any presents. We have to check them."

An alarm rang in her head. Startled, Gwen started to jerk back and was held firmly against him, his breath still hot on her ear.

"Don't pull away. Now get her away from the presents."

She drew a shaky breath then faced Ardelle with an award-winning grin. "Ardelle, don't you want to instruct Hillary about preparing afternoon tea for Levan? I do enjoy talking to him." Somehow she managed to say it convincingly.

Ardelle's disapproving scowl over their affection gave way to a surprised stare. "You do?"

"Oh, yes, he's so interesting. And we do want to know what the newest fashion will be before Bunny Hentford does."

Her sister grinned back with malicious pleasure. "Yes, we most certainly do." She dropped the package on to a cushion of the settee. "I'll be right back." Glancing backward at Trish, she jabbed a finger at the air and instructed, "Open that. I want to see what monstrosity Elise sent you."

For Jack she had only a quick, superficial, closed-lipped smile as she passed him.

Gwen waited until her sister disappeared from sight, then heaved a sigh. "Agony. Absolute agony," she muttered, looking up at Jack in a threatening manner. "You have no idea how boring that man is. Now, I have to sit through a lunch with him."

"Better than seeing your sister blown up."

Trish looked down at the package she'd picked up and dumbly let it tumble back to the cushion. Eyes wide with alarm, she jumped from her seat and backed away from it. "My God, Gwen."

"Calm down," she said sternly, trying to quiet her sister before Ardelle rushed back in. "He'll handle it." She said the words simply, casually. Only as she watched how carefully Jack picked up the present did the danger fully register in her mind. "You don't think that it's—"

Balancing the package on his fingertips, he passed her in the archway. "Don't let your sisters open any of these. I'll talk to Horton about delivering them to us first."

She nodded numbly, not realizing she was holding her breath until the front door closed behind him. Rather than relief, she felt a new kind of panic rise within her. She raced to the window to see where he was walking with the package. He was striding quickly toward the gardener's shed. When Earl hurried toward him, Jack raised his hand, signaling him to back off.

Sighing, Trish sidled closer and stared out the window with her. "Oh, Gwen, it couldn't be a—it could have blown up in Ardelle's hands."

"It could explode out there," Gwen responded softly, feeling something heavy pressing against her chest. She thought of the danger one man suddenly faced—the man she'd fallen in love with.

Fifteen minutes later, Gwen was standing on a chair playing pin cushion as Levan twisted and turned her, rattling on about his latest trip to Paris. Ardelle stood by approvingly. Trish squirmed restlessly on the Queen Anne chair in her bedroom. And Jack still hadn't emerged from the shed.

From her position before the bedroom window, Gwen could see Horton, standing like a sentry near the driveway, directing a deliveryman toward Earl. Earl, in turn, received the package and relayed it to another detective who then scurried it over to its final destination—the gardener's shed and the hands of Jack Mallory.

Gwen stood very still, listening, the chatter of her sisters drowned out by the pounding beat of her own

heart. She felt fear. It clung to her, played wild tricks
with her mind, jumbled her thoughts.

Outside, police detectives rushed around the gardener's shed, but no one entered. One man stayed
alone within it—one man risking his life for her family.

Unjustly, Gwen felt ready to scream in frustration
and annoyance at Levan and her sisters by the time
they finished the fitting session. Besides Trish, neither Ardelle nor Levan were aware of the possible
threat. And Trish, lovely Trish, could always be
counted upon to play ostrich.

Afternoon tea proved just as difficult to get
through, a petit four balling in Gwen's throat. When
it was finally time for him to leave, Levan, a breezy,
slightly built man, raked a hand through his shoul-
der-length hair and held Ardelle captive at the door for
several minutes.

Gwen heard Ardelle ooh agreeably to his procla-
mation that *the* fall color would be fuchsia. Unable to
stand it any longer, Gwen raced through the kitchen
and headed for the gardener's shed. Talk of a fuchsia
dress seemed ridiculous in comparison to what Jack
was facing.

Gwen got no closer than ten feet to the shed.

At that point, Earl rushed forward and blocked her
way. "You can't go in there."

She didn't try to veil her worry. "How is he doing?" But just as she asked the question Jack appeared in the doorway. She skirted around Earl to
meet him.

"Hey." Catching up with her, Earl grabbed her arm. "You can't go in."

Jolted to a stop, Gwen released a faint, annoyed sigh. She met his stare squarely and silently.

"Let her come in," Jack called out.

"Let her—" Earl shot him a baffled look, then shrugged and stepped aside.

Confusion seemed the order of the moment. Gwen took one step into the shed and stopped mid-stride, frozen by the sight before her.

"I need help," Jack said, his voice edged with something akin to amusement.

"Help? My God, what did you do?" she asked, unexpectedly feeling laughter rising within her.

"No bomb, but—" He gestured at the mass of wrapping paper and ribbon tossed in a corner. "I need someone to help me rewrap these."

"And I have the honor?"

"As my fiancé, aren't you supposed to be a help-mate?"

When she finally approached the workbench, he joined her, his shoulder brushing hers. "You're stretching this, Sergeant," she said, eyeing the packages piled on the bench. "You did keep the right cards with the right presents, didn't you?"

He coiled a strand of her hair around his finger. "Yeah, I did that."

She sighed with relief, thinking of Trish and her thank-you notes.

"You do know how to wrap a present, don't you? If not, maybe Hillary—"

Gwen drilled him with a withering look.

Reluctantly he let her hair slip through his fingers and gathered up the wrapping paper strewn across the workbench.

"No one will believe these came from such an expensive shop." She ran a smooth hand over a wrinkled white sheet decorated with pale pink bells.

"Play dumb. If you don't admit to knowledge of the crime, they can't get you."

She laughed and grabbed the scissors. "I thought you were an honest cop."

He frowned, looking affronted. "I am. But I would have been a smart crook, too."

"No, you wouldn't have. You're too honest." Something in the way he shrugged, eyes downcast, his silence, made Gwen sense he wasn't joking any longer. Somewhere she'd struck a sensitive nerve. She set the package in her hand aside and touched his cheek to force his attention back to her. "Why did you—"

He looked uneasy.

"Tell me," she urged. "Please, tell me what you were thinking."

"That I haven't been honest with you."

"About what?"

"My background." She remained silent; her eyes haunted him to talk. Vulnerable. For the first time in his life, he felt a vulnerability that he couldn't defend himself against. He damned himself and his own weakness even as he spoke. "I learned my mother was born in a small town in Texas. Few people even remembered her. She'd left the town when a spinster aunt had died."

He paused, too many memories flashing back, reminding him of how he'd once felt. Alone. So damn alone. At eighteen he'd yearned to have someone—anyone. "I went to her last known address. The landlady said that she hadn't known my mother well, but she was sweet—nice—but real quiet. She never had any visitors, but the woman remembered she'd mentioned a previous address."

"Did you go there?"

Jack looked away. It could have been yesterday instead of nearly seventeen years ago. "I was obsessed to find my father. Another tenant remembered my mother and the man who'd visited her a few times." He shook his head, speaking honestly. "I never did learn his name." He wanted to stop. Why had he begun dredging up a past that he'd nearly forgotten? He hadn't thought about that time in his life for years. And here he was, because of one woman's haunting blue eyes, exposing a pain he'd thought he'd long ago buried.

"Jack." She moved closer as if aware he planned to move away from her. "Share it with me," she said softly.

He stared at her hair, strands twisted from the wind. His life had felt just as entangled for years. "I was told that he was out of jail at the time. One of the few times in his life, I guess." Her eyes met his and he saw a question in them. What was she wondering? Who he was? He could answer that question. He was a cop. He'd found his family in the police force. He had no other ties. "But I learned he knew about me, knew and didn't stay around. I realized then that my mother had done me a favor by not telling me who he was. I'd led a better life without him than I would have had I known him."

"He doesn't matter anymore." She inched closer, linking her hand with his. "None of that matters. Who he was isn't nearly as important as who you are."

He stared down at the delicate hand wrapped around his. He couldn't recall anyone ever holding his hand just to assure him he wasn't alone. Hell, he'd always been alone until he'd joined the police force. Only then had he felt as if he belonged somewhere, as if he were bonded to any group of people.

At the sadness he saw in her eyes, his heart turned. He wanted to duck for cover as if a barrage of bullets were flying at him. But it was already too late. The target had been hit. She was offering what he'd never hoped to find. Love. "Your family—"

She set a finger to his lips to silence him. "*We* count, too, don't we?"

He wondered if she honestly believed that it was possible for them. Not wanting to say too much, he turned to leave.

A frown knitted her brow. "Aren't you going to help?" she asked. She didn't really care if he did or not, but she didn't want him to pull away from her again.

"Help?" he repeated, doubting she would ever realize how wonderfully giving she was.

"Help," she insisted, with exaggerated impatience. "You made the mess."

"I can't wrap."

"You'll learn."

Three presents later, she learned she was wrong. He was all thumbs. "I'll finish," she finally said, "but you stay." As he leaned his hip back against the workbench and grinned, it occurred to her that maybe he'd played helpless deliberately. "Put your finger here," she said, indicating a knot that she'd made with the ribbon. "Did you really expect to find a bomb?"

"We can't take any chances. And that one present ticked," he said, watching the slight flutter of her thick lashes. He smiled at her serious expression.

"Mrs. Farnsworth's gift. I should have warned you that she sends everyone a clock." Tying a bow, she went on. "Ardelle thinks Elise Farnsworth is a tight-wad. Two years ago, she received a clock from the Farnsworths. She's never forgiven them. She won't be happy to see this."

Shifting his stance to get closer, he skimmed a finger down the slender line of her neck. "Did they give you a hard time in there?"

Gwen kept taping the present. "Not any more than usual," she said, taking great pains to restore the wrapping to its elegant beginnings.

Hearing anxiety in her voice, Jack didn't buy her act of deep concentration. He placed his fingers beneath her chin and turned her face to him. "Do you know how you make me feel? How much I want to defend you from them?"

Some of the tenseness eased from her features. "Are you romancing me?"

Lightly he grazed her smiling lips. "Trying. But it really might not be good for you."

She faced him squarely and coiled her arms around his neck. "How can it be wrong when this feels so right?"

Jack hadn't been able to answer her question at the time, but at dinner, watching her strained smile, hearing her guarded words, he knew a woman as intelligent as she was wouldn't forever avoid seeing what was obvious. He didn't belong among them.

Beaming from across the table was a friend of Ardelle's, a snooty-looking woman with a soporific gaze and a saccharin smile. She wrote a chatty column for the newspaper's society page about the comings and goings of the suburban elite. Her attention was riveted on Jack at the present moment. "How utterly fascinating. A whirlwind romance sounds so wonderfully romantic, darling," she gushed at Gwen. "And the wedding will be?" Her voice raised expectantly, demanding an answer.

"We might elope," Jack returned, fed up with the woman's prying.

Looking down, Gwen veiled a smile while she pressed her knee hard against his.

Ardelle flushed crimson, her eyes blazing. "Jack is amusing you," she said quickly to her friend to prevent the woman from even considering the idea.

Beside her, Ralston glared. Jack expected at any moment to be challenged to a duel.

"Ashcrofts have always had traditional ceremonies, either at home or at Saint Luke's." Ardelle managed a laugh. "Elope. Such nonsense. Certain amenities must be observed."

Her friend's smile widened. "Oh," she responded, the monosyllable hanging in the air.

Jack dug a fork into the veal on his plate. Eat. Keep your mouth shut, and make it out of here safely, he told himself.

Within fifteen minutes, he was out the back door and following the path through the woods to the pond at the back of the estate.

Jamming a hand in his pants pocket, he stared at the water. The sight of it was soothing. Like it or not, he needed to face one fact. He would do her more harm than good. Ever since meeting her, he'd struggled to remember that, but every day, every moment, every second with her had made him dream. Until he'd met her, he hadn't realized how much he still ached for a family, for that special someone.

He stared out at the dark impenetrable woods. He saw nothing. For too many years, he'd felt nothing. Now he'd gone and done something foolish. He'd forgotten he was there to do a job and allowed himself to believe in a fantasy. And stupidly he'd fallen in love with her.

But no matter what he felt, the ending to all of this remained the same. He would leave. She would go on with her life. And in the end, she would fall in love with someone that the family found more acceptable.

The evening wind whipped around him. He turned his back to it and peered at his watch. He'd spent more time away from the house than he'd planned.

Head bent, he kept his eyes on his feet to dodge ruts in the path that led out of the woods. He knew now he couldn't tell her he loved her. He couldn't willingly disrupt her life, but neither could he deny wanting her. Right or wrong, he wanted whatever time he could have with her.

As the house came into view, he noted lights were still on. The wedding rehearsal was tomorrow. He felt desperate to spend as much time as he could with her.

Hurrying into the house and up the stairs, he felt impatient for moments with her, moments that he knew now couldn't last forever.

As he opened her bedroom door, slim, feminine arms snaked around his neck and yanked him inside. The room was dark.

Smiling, he felt the familiarity of her soft feminine body against his, heard a recognizable sensuality in her voice. "I thought you'd never get up here."

"Miss me?" As he drew back, even beneath the mantle of darkness, he could see the intense longing in her eyes. "It's a busy day for you tomorrow."

"Uh-huh."

He looked down to unbutton her blouse. "You need your sleep."

"Oh, yes," she said on a long breath as his knuckles grazed her flesh. "We have a day with the Bowmans, Wesley's parents."

"I won't be there."

Through hooded lids, Gwen met his stare while tugging his shirt from his jeans. "You will be there," she said in a playfully threatening tone.

"Can't."

The simple word brought forth the full weight of the danger to her father that might mar any moment. She tensed. As his hands stilled and his eyes fixed on hers, Gwen regretted giving herself away.

"What is it?" he asked with concern.

"You'll be checking the deliverymen?" At his nod, she considered her own dilemma. "What excuse will I give for your not being there?"

He bent his head and nipped her earlobe. "Tell them I'm allergic to the flowers in the garden."

She tried to ride his humor. "Lame. Really lame, Mallory. I'll look for you." Her hand crept down his thigh.

As her fingers dipped to his crotch, Jack laughed. "Okay, okay, I'll try to be there," he said in a voice thick with emotion.

Suddenly impatient, needing the strength and warmth of his body against hers, she popped the snap of his jeans.

"In a hurry?" he asked, a touch unevenly as he scooped her into his arms.

She laughed softly, tightening her hands around his neck, entwining her fingers in the thick hair falling over the collar of his shirt. "As much as you are."

Even before he lowered her to the bed, Gwen was curling her arms and legs around him. When she'd opened the door to him, she'd seen a brooding look in his eyes. Her need was great to ease away his troubled thoughts.

Whispery kisses quickly became deeper. She tasted a wild insistence in his mouth; his hands, struggling to be gentle, flirted with a bruising urgency.

Lips clung together a moment longer. Then his mouth moved everywhere, his voice ragged as he cursed his own clothing, and she heard the thunder of her own heart urging her to hurry him even more.

She wanted to tempt and torment and pleasure, but her desperation matched his. Greedily she touched him, reveling in the sleekness of his bare shoulders and the bunching muscles in his back, drawing him closer to her, needing the lips that urged hers, the tongue that probed.

There was no gentleness this time. He couldn't give it. She didn't want it. She threw her head back, pressing it into the pillow beneath her as his lips followed his hands in a blazing trail. Wherever he touched, her nerves tingled. Wherever his mouth caressed, her body glowed.

She fed on his excitement. Give. Please him. It was all she wanted. She closed her eyes and ran her hands over him, trying to memorize every inch of his lean body. She molded herself to the strong, callused hands gliding across her breasts, down her belly, between her thighs. Wild with wanting, she arched her body against his, urging him. His every touch, his every kiss, made her feel as if she'd never known love before. As if she never would again with another, she realized as each breath she took grew more ragged.

He murmured something soft, something unintelligible. Words didn't matter. Willingly, invitingly, she took him to her and closed her eyes to everything but the burning need engulfing her. Had she ever wanted, needed like this before? Would she ever feel that she'd had enough of him?

She wanted to speak, tell him how she felt. But reality slipped away. Breathless, she could only moan with him, rock against him. They led each other to one peak after another. And she shuddered—caught up in the madness and contentment, and the love she felt for him.

Minutes passed. Yet it seemed time had stopped. Slowly she drifted back down from some unearthly cloud until she was conscious of the dampness of flesh, of the harsh breaths in her ear, of the thudding beat of his heart matching her own.

"I needed you," he managed breathlessly.

Needed, not wanted, Gwen mused, clutching him fiercely to her. Love was *need* not want. She inhaled the scent of him, her fingers grazing over the tightness of his buttocks to keep him near when he began to lift himself from her. "Not yet," she insisted softly. "Not yet."

"Can you breathe?"

Eyes closed, she skimmed his back with her fingertips. "It isn't important."

"What is?" he asked against the curve of her neck.

She drew a hard breath to answer him. "You," she whispered. As he rolled her over with him, tangling a leg with hers and snuggling her closer, she felt as if he were wrapping her in a cocoon, a safe haven. And she accepted that being with him had brought that one emotion back to her. Without doubts, without fear of being hurt, she ached to love once more.

## Chapter Eleven

"I wonder what I'll look like later today," Gwen murmured.

Jack dragged on his jeans then dropped back to the bed and bent forward for his shoes. As he straightened, he caught a glimpse of Gwen scrunching her nose at her reflection.

"I'm off to Ardelle's favorite hair salon," she said, skimming his shoulder with a fingertip. "Philippe's." He smiled at her French accent. "I wish—" Her voice trailed off as he turned, bracketed her shoulders with his arms and poised over her. "I wish that we could stay here."

He drew a deep breath against her lips. "Never being satisfied is supposed to be good for the soul."

Gwen nipped at his bottom lip. "I don't think so."

He eased away from her and snatched up his shirt. "It's comforting to know that you'll be as miserable as I'll be." His words reminded him of a time that was drawing near. He'd leave soon. And, hell, yes, he'd be miserable. Miserable without her bright smiles, the sound of her voice, the gentleness of her caresses.

Silent and staring at him with eyes he could lose himself in, she sat on the edge of the bed, one slim thigh peeking out from the opening of her robe. As she rose slowly from the bed and ambled toward him, he thought she looked as if she'd stepped out of a magazine ad for an alluring perfume. She certainly did a number on him. In the green robe, her red hair draping her shoulders, the morning sunlight slicing a golden glow across her skin, she made him think of bright days, of warm nights, of forever. Sunshine. She was the sunshine that had been missing from his life, he realized.

"Where were you?" she teased at his quietness, brushing a fingertip across the fair hair above the V of his shirt.

Though her caress was feather-light, Jack felt heat blaze through him. "You make leaving impossible." He caught her hand and kissed her quickly. "I have to go."

Not giving himself time to reconsider, he moved out the door. He hadn't wanted to leave. He hadn't wanted to walk out of her room. Most of all, he hadn't wanted to end the make-believe world he'd entered ever since that special night.

At six in the morning the house was quiet, eerily so. Jack made his way to the kitchen, had some coffee, then walked outside. The closer it got to the wedding, the more on alert everyone had to be.

Lighting a cigarette, he thought back to the previous night. For a few hours, he'd forgotten everything, including the threats and the uncertainty of a future with her. But morning always swept away those moonlit moments. What was impossible became clear at daybreak. He was reminded of the gap between the life she'd known and the life he could offer her.

Glancing around him, he saw Earl standing by the family limo. A rag in his hand, he wiped at the top of the hood. "Keep up the good work," Jack gibed, "and they might really hire you."

Earl waved away the remark, dropped the rag, and dug into his pants pocket. "Look at this," he muttered, waving a sheet of paper at Jack. "This is my schedule today. Hairdresser. Lingerie shop. And there are a half dozen other places I have to drive Trish Ashcroft to today."

"You didn't want to trade with Lyndon," Jack reminded him, before taking a drag on his cigarette.

"Hell, no. I thought the bride-to-be would be easier to guard than her father."

"Nothing will be easy today or tomorrow."

Earl nodded, glancing at his watch. "Yeah, no rest all day."

Jack's smile deepened when Gwen emerged from the house. He considered how much easier his assignment had been than Earl's. But then, he'd stopped viewing his time with her as a job almost from the beginning.

Her eyes bright with humor, she placed a finger to the edges of her lips and curved them upward in a phony smile. "I'm ready for Philippe's magic fingers."

"Tough assignment," Earl mumbled low.

Ignoring him, Jack dropped his cigarette and approached her. "Just so they're not too magical."

She laughed. It was a soft, husky laugh that aroused him as easily as her kisses did, but neither her smile nor his attempt at humor relaxed him today. She was going to be around too many strangers. "Stay there," he insisted. "I'll bring the car around."

She paused on one of the steps and sent him a puzzled look. "I'll walk with you."

Jack shook his head. "No. It's too dangerous. If Fred can get in without being stopped, so can someone else," he said simply as an explanation.

He saw a flicker of fear in her eyes at what he wasn't saying. In its wake was a look of frustration at the lack of freedom imposed on her. Then almost stubbornly, she seemed to force a faint smile. A smile meant to send a clear message of trust, and he realized what she was really offering him. If a man's legs could weaken from a single look, his would have at that moment.

By the time they returned to the house, afternoon sunlight bleached the sky. Gwen went in and Jack watched the door close behind her. He was like a man facing an impenetrable wall. When he was alone with her, nothing else mattered. The problem was they weren't always alone. No one lived in a vacuum.

She had a throng of highbrow relatives and acquaintances who would never let him forget his place. There was the cousin she'd met at the salon, the one with the flashy diamond. The woman had chattered about her second husband, some count with relatives from a place Jack had never heard of. Regardless of what he and Gwen felt, her social standing, her wealth, her family name were wedged firmly between them. He crushed his cigarette with his heel and rounded the side of the house.

Huddled with Lyndon and another detective, Earl beckoned to him. "Caulder just called." A weariness crept into his voice. "They got a tip. The hit is on for today or tomorrow."

Jack felt slow. A moment passed before he repeated, "They got a tip?"

A quick visual exchange passed between him and Earl, nothing more.

Jack kept walking, pondering the information. He knew how the department worked. They had used people as bait before. If there was an informant, then protecting the Ashcrofts was part of some plan, a plan that was using them to catch Farrow.


Gwen stood before a mirror in the foyer and tugged at a curl. The hairdo was too fussy to suit her. Turning toward the stairs, she suddenly heard voices drifting through the opened terrace doors and did an about-face.

Sitting on the patio with his coffee and the *Wall Street Journal,* her father wasn't alone. Perched on the edge of the chair next to him, Ardelle hunched forward with an annoyed expression on her face. Gwen guessed her father was being told about her obstinacy regarding the dance studio, maybe even being reminded that Gwen hadn't chosen the right man.

Squaring her shoulders, Gwen marched forward, deciding she deserved her time in court, too. Determined to take control, she smiled with the enthusiasm of a toothpaste model. "Oh, good, coffee," she said breezily. "When are Wesley and his family arriving?"

"Soon," Ardelle answered, tilting her head. She stared at Gwen's hair. "Philippe certainly works wonders."

"Just marvy," she answered, reaching for the carafe on the table. To her father she said, "I'd like time to talk to you."

Ardelle sent their father a meaningful stare, snapped to a stand and departed.

Gwen sank to the chair her sister had vacated, waiting until Ardelle was out of sight to begin speaking. "I guess you've been told how impossible I am."

Smiling wanly, he refolded his newspaper. "It isn't the first time."

Her stomach turned, but she leveled a stare at him. "I'm not giving up the dance studio."

"I knew that when you opened it."

Gwen stared dumbly at him. "You don't object?"

"Your mother would be pleased."

Why hadn't she asked him before? she wondered. Afraid. She'd been afraid they would argue, afraid she would lose him again. She touched his hand resting on the arm of the chair. "I really was worried."

A surprised look of disbelief crossed his face. "Am I such an ogre?"

She couldn't help smiling. "No, not an ogre," she said honestly. "Stodgy, just stodgy."

He was silent as if considering the description. "There are worse things to be, I suppose."

Gwen laughed genuinely. "Yes, much worse," she said, bending forward to kiss his cheek. She pulled back quickly, as surprised by the demonstrative gesture as he seemed to be. Feeling awkward, she settled back with a self-conscious smile.

He cleared his throat. "I—uh—wish I could keep this happy moment going but we need to talk. You and Detective Mallory—" He paused, looking uncharacteristically at a loss for words. "You were quick to come to his defense the other morning when I questioned where he'd been."

Gwen shifted uncomfortably. "You were bellowing. The whole family nearly learned who he really is. That wouldn't do, would it?"

"No," he agreed easily. "Neither Ardelle nor Ralston do well under stress. And she would tell your aunt, who seems unable to control her mouth," he said, appearing baffled by the condition. "And then Farrow would know. Any protection we have would be undermined." Looking down, he glanced at his wristwatch.

She'd seen him give such a signal a hundred times while growing up. Its meaning was clear. She had five minutes of time. No more.

"You were wise to stop me then. But now is different. I want to know where he was."

Gwen decided it was time to take the bull by the horns. "With me," she stated.

He looked comically perplexed. "With you?" he repeated. "Gwen—"

"Don't, Father. I know what I'm doing."

"And what is that?"

"I love him."

He drew back as if suddenly hit by a sharp pain. "You can't possibly mean that."

"Oh, yes, I do."

"You don't know him."

"He's with me practically twenty-four hours a day. I've seen him angry, worried—hurt. I've laughed with him and wanted to cry for him. I care what happens to him," she insisted.

Slowly he shook his head, as if muddled and trying to grasp some rational thought. "I never expected this. But you have to realize that he has a different life-style. You know nothing about it."

"Yes, I do. I've seen where he lives." Though he arched a brow in surprise, she went on steadily. "I know what gives him joy. I like Earl—Detective Kowalski—his best friend. We like greasy hamburgers and sailing and—" She stopped, realizing that none of those things mattered, that he'd be glancing at his wristwatch again in another second. "We have more in common than you'd expect."

"Even so—"

She pushed herself upright, ready to leave before he made the request.

"Sit back down," he insisted.

"But you're busy and—"

"Busy! I'm not too busy for my daughter. I never have been," he said in angry defense. "Now, tell me. Does he love you?"

"Love me?" she mumbled inanely.

He frowned. "Don't forget that our money is attractive, Gwen."

She squirmed, uneasy with the direction he was taking. "It isn't to him. I don't think he'd want it—or anything—from me."

Her father didn't look convinced. "Everyone has their price."

Gwen willed herself to stay seated. "Ardelle believes that, too. I don't."

"Despite all you've said, you do still have a problem. He isn't used to this, Gwen," he said, gesturing at their surroundings.

"Neither was mother, but she adjusted."

Concern deepened some of the lines in his face. "Not really." Then a slip of smile softened his expression. "She endured for my sake."

"So it's possible, isn't it? It's possible for such a love to work."

He averted his eyes as if uncomfortable. "I don't want you unhappy again."

Her tone was pleading in response. "Some of the best people lack an ounce of blue blood. Like mother," she added. "The blood mixed well, didn't it. We didn't come out purple."

He couldn't help but laugh.

Gwen smiled instinctively in response, then drew a deep, steadying breath. "You'd accept him, wouldn't you?"

He pushed back his chair to stand, then offered his hands to her. "You remind me so of your mother. When she wanted something, she picked away until I forgot my arguments, until I wanted to see only one thing." He studied Gwen and then said softly, "Her smile."

Gwen raised bright eyes to him, gave him the smile that he wanted.

"Not everyone will be so understanding," he reminded her.

"You mean Ardelle and Ralston—and Aunt Ursula?"

He smiled wryly. "As I've always done, I'll handle them, though," he said with complete confidence. Then he shifted his eyes and looked past her.

Aware of his distraction, Gwen turned around to see Wesley approaching. She felt her good mood wavering. The wedding rehearsal seemed like a countdown toward a disastrous event.

As her father hooked her arm with his, she was reminded that Ashcroft blood ran through her veins. Though she didn't always offer the expected pleasantries, she had learned them well. And this was a time to use them. Brightly she smiled at Wesley's parents, trailing their son as if he were a crown prince. Within minutes, all of the wedding party had gathered.

Bronte, wife of Wesley's megabucks brother, waved her hand as if she were a traffic cop in downtown Chicago. As was expected of her, Gwen politely commented on the woman's new diamond ring.

"We were so thrilled that our Wesley and your Trish would be a cozy twosome." She delivered her lines in an upper-crust tone that grated on Gwen.

Nearby Wesley complained loudly. "You would think people could be on time."

"Only the minister isn't here," Trish said from behind a wooden smile.

"I hope he comes soon." Wesley pushed back the cuff of his shirtsleeve and peered at his watch. "I need to return to the office."

Standing beside him, Trish looked away, blinking fast.

He gave her a perfunctory kiss on the cheek. "To take our honeymoon, I have to work extra hard today," he excused himself. "I won't be able to stay long at the rehearsal dinner. You understand." He said it as if it were a fact.

Gwen wanted to kick the insensitive dope.

On the other side of Gwen, Bronte played a verbal game of financial one-upmanship with Ardelle about vacations recently taken.

"Of course," Bronte said reflectively, "So much traveling does promote domestic problems. We are having a terrible crisis with the help."

Ardelle murmured sweetly, "How terrible. You should talk to Bunny Hentford," she advised, steering Bronte toward her arch-enemy who repeatedly showed atrocious taste in choosing her servants. "She has wonderful help. Perhaps she'll give you the name of the agency she uses."

As Bronte went on about some relative of English nobility who would attend the wedding, Gwen plunged her hands into her skirt pockets. Finally the minister arrived. The sooner they started, the sooner it would be over.

"What a circus." Earl scowled, lumbering toward Jack as he stood near the front door. The soft strains of a harpsichord drifted on the air. "I like the music though. Is he practicing what he'll play tomorrow?"

"Guess so," Jack answered absently. The music for tomorrow's wedding wasn't on his mind. Ever since he'd learned about the department's plan, he'd been uneasy.

Everything he'd valued seemed on the line. His job had always provided the only family he'd ever known. A person knew the quirks of family members. So why hadn't he guessed what Caulder was up to?

Dumb question. Deep down, he must have known they were using the family as bait and had dodged the truth. Why? Why hadn't he wanted to face it?

He was his father's son after all, Jack thought, sighing disgustedly. Hadn't he always believed his father had betrayed him and his mother by looking away—just as he'd done in protecting the Ashcrofts—in loving Gwen? Blood of his blood, flesh of his flesh.

He cursed silently, aware that he hadn't wanted to face the truth. He had lied to himself with thoughts about not being able to offer Gwen the kind of life she was used to. He wondered if his own father had used similar thoughts to dodge love. Making a commitment to someone was the one unselfish act his father hadn't been able to do. And though Jack knew he loved Gwen, he hadn't done the one thing necessary to prove it. He hadn't made a commitment to her. If he had, he would have leveled with her, but some part of him had held on to a deception he'd refused to see until now.

Glancing toward the house, he wondered where she was. A few moments alone with her was all he needed to tell her the truth, the whole truth. "Look, I'll be right back."

Earl snapped a frown at him, "Huh?"

"I'll be back," Jack said, already striding toward the back of the house. As the minister gave instructions to Trish and Wesley, he waited until everyone's attention was focused on them, then stepped close to Gwen.

"You came," she said quietly, looking pleased.

"Come with me," he insisted, slipping his fingers over her arm.

She looked up at him uncertainly. "I can't leave yet."

"Just for a minute."

Gwen glanced around her. Though she guessed someone would lambaste her for sneaking away, she couldn't ignore the urgency in his voice. "I can only be away for a minute," she said, when they stepped past the terrace doors and into her father's study.

"Listen." His hands were tight on her upper arms, as if he were afraid she would flee.

Gwen wanted to smile but he looked too serious. "What's wrong?"

"Nothing. Everything is finally all right. I love you," he said softly.

She felt her legs weaken. "What?"

"I love you," he repeated. "I honestly didn't want to care so much about you," he said, disturbed by his own words. "I didn't want to complicate everything between us, but I can't go on not telling you what you mean to me, not admitting that I've been—I've been afraid." The word stuck in his throat. "Afraid of commitment to anyone."

She made a small sound as he crushed her to him.

For a moment, he just held her. "I've been dumb," he said, rearing back to see her face. "I've had something with you I've never known before."

"Jack." Lightly she touched his jaw to reassure him that love was all she yearned for from him.

"No." He shook his head. "I need to say more. I need to tell you that whatever you give up for me—I'll make it up to you. I'll love you like no other man ever could."

She melted against him. "I'll hold you to that promise, Sergeant. I love you, too."

"Gwen?"

At her sister's voice, she forced herself to pull away from him. "I have to go."

"Wait a minute."

She laughed as he drew her back. "I can't," she said lightly, then kissed him hard. "Later."

Jack strolled back to the front of the house. He should have felt like the luckiest man in the world, but he was still worried. He should have told her everything.

At the sound of a truck door, he snapped himself back to his job and followed the movement of two deliverymen carrying in cases of champagne. An entourage from the catering service trailed them. Jack glanced at the list of names on a clipboard in Earl's hand. "They were all checked?" he asked, knowing he couldn't take time for any more distractions until all the deliveries were made.

"Yep. We got a clearance on everyone. Our men have checked every bottle, every deliveryman, every vehicle, every type of food and every damn flower."

Jack didn't doubt he'd been thorough. After the slipup about the gifts, Earl's pride demanded he not make another oversight.

"Ashcroft shouldn't be here while the workmen are setting up the tents," he said with a trace of annoyance.

Nearby, two workmen struggled to maneuver an arched trellis past the line of delivery trucks. One cussed the other as he let the trellis slip and the edge of it came down on the toe of his sneakers. The stream of expletives were abruptly replaced with a flush of embarrassment as the workman saw the minister.

Playing deaf, he nodded in passing on his way to his car.

Jack glanced toward the front door, expecting to see Gwen now that the rehearsal was over. "What time are they doing the final setup tomorrow?"

"Right after dawn. Some things about this assignment aren't too bad," Earl said. "I already sampled the caviar. No strychnine in it. It tasted great."

"Too rich for my tastes." Jack's response was drowned out by a loud clatter behind them. In what appeared a choreographed movement, he and Earl whipped around to the sight of white folding chairs sprawled on the walkway.

As a grumbling workman bent over the fallen chairs, Earl released a hard breath. "Damn. I wish I had more eyes." His voice trailed off, his gaze shifting to a dark Oldsmobile coming up the driveway.

For the past five years Jack had been Earl's partner. Messages often were exchanged in silence. Jack understood his questioning look. The car was an unmarked police-department vehicle.

Together they took a step toward the man rounding the front of the car. A big man, bullnecked and meticulously groomed, their captain claimed to be a by-the-book man, but he was known to bend the rules. A shrewd man, he believed in the adage that the end justified the means. As the breeze ruffled thin, gray strands on his head, annoyance crossed his craggy face. He met Jack and Earl halfway, stopping at the edge of the walkway that led to the front door. "You got my message?"

"We got it." An uneasiness spread through Jack. "You have an informant?"

"We've had him from day one."

"Day one of this?" Jack's answer was more critique than question. Beside him, Earl did a nervous dance in place. Jack knew his voice had tightened with anger, but he didn't give a damn. "Is the department paying this person?"

"You know how it works," the captain said, too amiably to suit Jack. "He's one of Farrow's men who's trying to save his neck on a charge against him. He'll get immunity for helping us." He cocked his head, his eyes narrowing. "What's your problem, Mallory?"

"Why didn't we know about this?" Jack demanded.

"It wasn't necessary," Caulder said matter-of-factly. "We want Farrow on an attempted-murder conspiracy. Ashcroft will be safe, so who's hurt?" Without waiting for a response, he turned away and returned to his car. But even if he'd wanted an answer, he wouldn't have gotten one.

Jack's attention had already shifted from him. Every anxious moment he'd had since learning about the real plan closed in on him. There was Gwen, standing near enough to have overheard. And the look in her eyes was disbelief.

Why now? Jack wanted to yell, certain she'd heard something. Why hadn't he been given just a few more minutes to tell her that he hadn't known any of it until minutes ago.

As he made his way to her, she stared blankly at him, her eyes void of expression. "Whatever you heard—"

"Don't," she said softly. "Please, don't lie anymore. You're using us?"

She'd never understand, he realized. She was focused on one thought—one thought only. He'd been part of a plan that had used her and her family. He was no different than so many others she'd made the mistake of caring about. He tried to explain. "It's not exactly that way."

Pale, she curled her fingers into her palms. "Just part of your job?" She didn't wait for his response.

"How could you tell me you loved me? You aren't any different than the others, are you? You didn't want money or to use our name to your advantage but you certainly used all of us—in a different way."

Her accusations chilled him. "It wasn't for me."

"For the police department?"

"Yeah," he said emphatically. "For them."

Sadness clung to her voice. "You and they are one and the same."

As she turned around to walk away, he snagged her wrist but doubted he could reason with her. "Why the hell does it make a difference that you didn't know everything?" he asked, looking for some way to stop what was happening.

"Because of trust." She hurled the words furiously. "I might not always like my family, but I love them. You didn't care if any of them were hurt." Her voice was laced with harsh pain. "All you cared about was getting Farrow."

He reached forward but hesitated, certain she would shun his touch. "I'm sorry that it came out this way, but—" He paused in response to the sound of footsteps clicking on the driveway and swung a look up from the man's polished shoes to his face. The workman offered an apologetic look for interrupting them. Jack stepped aside to let him pass.

"Don't apologize to me, Jack," she practically begged, backing away. "Don't worry." Her words came out whispery. "I won't ruin your plans. I'll let you use me one more time. I'll play the loving fiancé so you can catch the bad man. For my father, I'll do that." She took another step from him as if needing distance. "You always said we were wrong for each other." Her fingers tightened on the stem of the glass she held. "You were right." Her voice grew stronger. "I trusted you. I thought that I'd met the one person in this world who would be honest with me, who wouldn't deceive me. I believed you when you said you loved me. But you don't understand love. You don't know how to think about anyone but yourself."

Her words cut with a sharpness he'd never expected. As he stared at eyes, dark and moist with anger and hurt, his own anger rose to defend himself.

Two more workmen stood near, shuffling their feet impatiently and waiting for them to move. Annoyance fluttered inside Jack. When he stepped to the side to let them pass with the heavy tent equipment, she sidestepped him the other way.

Jack didn't try to stop her. He knew denial would be useless. He couldn't blame her for believing he was guilty.

"Trouble?" Earl asked, suddenly beside him.

Jack didn't meet his stare. "I let her down." As a kid, he'd wanted a lot of things. A home, a family, a normal childhood. He'd never had them. He couldn't change that. People didn't always get what they wanted. But he wondered if he'd ever get the image of her now—so pale, her eyes so haunted—out of his mind.

"You love her, huh?"

"Too much," he admitted, forcing himself to concentrate on the trucks parked in the driveway. An uneasiness slithered through him as something he couldn't name suddenly gnawed at him. "Check the registration on that truck," he insisted and whipped around. He wasn't aware he was striding toward Gwen until he was steps from her. Blocking her path to the door, Ardelle was haranguing her for failing to do something.

Gwen reached for a calmness that was as fragile as the crystal in her hand. Her sister's voice was like a distant echo, her words running together as if she were speaking a foreign language. Too many thoughts, too many emotions, mingled in her head. She had to consciously draw a breath. "You were looking for me?" she asked, focusing on her sister. Pride—a smidgen of it was all she had left—demanded that she not lose control.

Ardelle craned her neck to see past Gwen.

From her sister's deepening frown, Gwen knew Jack was within inches. Pain and humiliation clawed at her. She was such a fool. Stupid, gullible Gwen. Every man she'd ever cared about had had ulterior motives.

She swallowed hard, wanting to cry, realizing she still wanted him to open his arms and tell her that she'd heard all wrong. But nothing he said would erase the distrust. She fought the tightness in her throat. If he touched her now, if he forced the pretense on her, she would fold. Don't touch me. Please, don't touch me. She wanted to yell it.

Ardelle sighed heavily. "I realize that you're one-minded these days, but are you even interested in knowing what's happening?" At Gwen's mechanical nod, she raised her voice again, letting her own irritation slide out. "We have a problem." She waved a bag in the air. "The wrong shoes were sent to us." Her look said she was waiting for Gwen's response.

What did she want from her? Gwen tried to concentrate. "Shoes? The wrong shoes?"

"Yes, the wrong—"

Close behind her, Jack echoed only one of their words. "Shoes!"

Gwen whipped around, her stomach tensing at the alarm she'd heard in his voice. He was already running toward the back of the house, toward her father. As he hurdled the wall then disappeared, fear rose within her. She didn't give herself time to think.

The glass in her hand shattering on the cement, she raced after him, brushing shoulders with a detective. Behind her she heard Ardelle yelling, but Gwen couldn't stop. Panic clenched her throat.

Winded, Earl shouted words that confirmed her fear. "One workman too many!" He waved frantically for several detectives to charge in from the wooded area.

*One workman in polished Italian leather shoes.* Gwen recalled the clicking of his heels on the driveway.

Agonizing for her father's safety, for Jack's, she wanted to scream, yell at everyone to stop. No one would—not her father who was turning around like a revolving target to see what was causing commotion behind him, not the workman who was pulling out a gun, not Jack who was diving at it.

## Chapter Twelve

A shot resounded in the air. Jack staggered as white-hot pain seared his shoulder. He felt the wet heat of blood seeping from it, a weakness floating over him. He heard the high-pitched screams of hysteria, then Earl's voice. He was on the ground, straining to sit up, straining to find Gwen. He could see her in his mind, and for a second, he thought he heard her voice, heard her calling his name. He wanted to cling to the sound, but it faded. And damn, he knew he was going to do something dumb. He was going to pass out.

No one questioned Gwen when she insisted on going to the hospital. After all, he was still her fiancé. Only a few people knew that everything had been a pretense between her and Jack.

She sat in the hospital waiting room, staring down the long white corridor, an antiseptic smell enveloping her with each breath she drew.

At the end of the corridor, Earl rocked back on his heels outside the room they'd wheeled Jack into. He'd quickly reassured her when she'd arrived. "He regained consciousness in the ambulance. They're removing the bullet now, but the doc says he'll keep him here for a day or two." With the same protectiveness he'd shown toward Trish throughout the past weeks, he'd led her by the elbow down the corridor. But while she had sat, he had paced.

She didn't move from the chair, couldn't. And she couldn't switch off the love she felt for Jack. Hands clenched, her head pounding dully, she stared out the window of the hospital at the darkening sky.

As time crept along, night shrouding the trees and shrubs around the hospital, she clung to positive thoughts. He wasn't hurt badly. He'd been rushed without delay to the hospital. He'd be able to go home soon.

"They're moving him to a room."

Startled, she jumped, amazed she hadn't heard Earl's approaching footsteps on the white-tiled floor.

He leaned forward and placed a comforting hand on her shoulder. "He's all right," he assured her, his voice calm.

Gwen took her first relaxing breath in hours. "He's really all right?" she asked, needing further guarantees.

He offered her a lopsided grin. "He's not soft."

She'd never thought he was. Jack had never hid the tough no-nonsense aspect of his character. But beneath it, she'd thought she had seen a softer man, a gentler one, someone who understood that love and honesty went hand in hand. "Thank you for telling me," she said to Earl.

"The doc said he could go home in a couple of days."

Gwen nodded, then forced herself to stand. As emotions warred inside her, she willed herself toward the door.

Earl did a double step and caught up with her. "You're coming back, aren't you?" He touched her arm, preventing her from reaching for the door handle. "To talk to him?"

Gwen looked down, avoiding his beseeching frown. "We've talked," she said quietly. "There is nothing else to say."

Drifting clouds shadowed the morning sunlight. Restless, Jack was dressed before the doctor arrived in his room. He had no intention of staying in the hospital any longer than he had to.

"This is dumb. What harm would there be in staying a couple more days?" Earl asked.

Jack struggled to dress, slipping one arm into the sleeve of a blue chambray shirt. The other sleeve hung limply at his side, the shirt draped over a shoulder and a bulky sling.

"Really dumb, Mallory," Earl insisted, trailing him to the nurses' station.

Jack shrugged in answer, impatient for his final release papers. He wanted to go home. *Home.* Why did
the word seem even more meaningless now than ever
before?

From the moment he entered his apartment, his
imagination kept flashing back to one special rainy
night. He kept seeing Gwen, hearing her laugh, her
soft moan when she'd pressed against him while they'd
made love.

Earl lingered in the doorway. "Want me to stick
around?"

"Go home. Louise has probably forgotten what you
look like."

Earl didn't move. "She's used to me being away."

"Go home," Jack urged. "I'll be all right."

He heard the click of the door closing behind Earl
and then silence. Years of unbearable loneliness
swarmed back over him.

A pain spiraled through him that cut deeper than
any bullet could. For the first time in his life, he knew
the agony of missing someone, of caring about someone, of worrying about that person more than one-
self. He felt desperate to hear Gwen's voice, to see her.

He was on his way into the bedroom when the
doorbell rang. For a split second, he dropped his
guard, told himself it was her.

Instead a delivery boy stood before him. Mechani-
cally, Jack accepted the package. With one hand, he
tore the brown paper away. The ache inside him in-
tensified as he stared at the painting, Gwen's paint-

ing—a sailboat heading toward the dock before the storm hit.

On a curse, Jack sank to a chair and agonized, as he faced his own fears straight-on for the first time in his life. She had said that he didn't know how to care about anyone but himself. At one time that had been true. But it wasn't the truth anymore. And the fact that it wasn't made the thought of a future without her unbearable.

He was going insane, he thought, running a hand over the stubble on his jaw. Leaning forward, an elbow on his thigh, he stared down at the floor. Without her, he'd have nothing—like before he met her. Without her, he'd be alone forever.

A drizzling rain had fallen during the night, but the morning sunlight peeked out from behind clouds and glared through Gwen's bedroom window. Last night, she'd convinced herself that the void in her heart would disappear. She'd sent Jack the painting, unable to look at it and not be haunted by painful memories.

But she awoke thinking of him, worrying about him. In the middle of brushing her teeth, she yearned for the sound of his voice.

Quickly she slipped on a jogging suit and sneakers. For a few moments, she needed time alone before the house crowded with guests for the wedding.

Hurrying down the stairs, she heard the sound of voices drifting from the dining room. Gwen reached the foyer without being noticed, but then her father's words halted her mid-stride.

"So all of them were here for protection," he explained casually, underplaying the threats.

"And he wasn't really Gwen's fiancé?" Ardelle asked, almost breathless.

God, she wasn't prepared for this, Gwen realized, leaning against the small foyer table.

"No, he wasn't."

"But she seemed—"

Her father cut in to stop his oldest daughter's speculation. "The police have informed me that they arrested John Farrow at three o'clock this morning."

Gwen said a silent, thankful prayer that he was finally safe.

"They're keeping a few men posted as a precaution, but the danger is practically nonexistent now."

"This is all so utterly awful," Ardelle murmured. "Ralston and I never guessed—"

"No, we didn't," Ralston piped in irritably. "I do wish you had told us."

"For everyone's safety, silence was the best way," her father assured them.

Murmurs of reluctant agreement rounded the table.

As Horton passed her in the foyer, Gwen raised a silencing finger to her lips. Dutifully he nodded, then paused in the archway to announce to the family the arrival of the photographer and videographers.

Gwen chose the moment to run out the door. Running usually helped her relax, work off frustration, disappointment, anger. But she quickly discovered it wasn't the cure for a broken heart. By the time she retraced her steps back to the house, she wasn't even sure she'd be able to manage the right smiles at the right moments.

Within the hour, dark clouds had gathered, and canvas was flapping beneath a strong breeze. Giggles floated through the hallway as several of Trish's bridesmaids arrived. Gwen fingered her dress, a dusty-peach gown of crepe and lace. Determined to get through the day, she snatched up the matching broad-brimmed hat and opened the door.

Strolling outside past the back door, she was met by nonstop activity as the caterer barked instructions to three men carrying a multitiered wedding cake.

She heard a car engine and glanced toward the sound to see an old sportscar braking at the end of the line of Mercedeses and Rolls-Royces and Cadillacs. She froze as she watched Jack emerge from a blue Corvette. Why had he come back? She didn't want to see him again. Not ever again, she told herself, even as her gaze swept longingly over him. Concern fluttered inside her at the sight of the white sling contrasting starkly against his dark suit. As he approached her, she searched his eyes for tiredness or pain. "What are you doing here?"

"I had unfinished business to take care of," he said in a too familiar firm tone.

"Business with my father?" she asked, wondering what else the police could want.

"With you."

"We don't have anything else to say to each other."

"Like hell we don't," he cut in quickly, then looked away as if annoyed with himself for losing control.

"This time you're going to listen." He drew a hard breath. "About what happened with your father, we— I should have realized what was happening but—"

Nervously she brushed back tendrils of hair flying across her face. "You did what you had to do."

The coolness in her voice cut through him. "I didn't do anything," he said in a fierce, yet soft tone. "I didn't use you. Maybe I was blind. Maybe I should have guessed that something was going on. But I didn't. I don't have any excuse except that I wasn't thinking straight about anything but protecting you."

"Wonderful way you have of protecting me. It always amazes me how people can justify lying," she said with finality before whirling away.

She had taken only one step when he caught her wrist. "Dammit, listen to me."

Her heart jumped and Gwen had to fight the urge to turn into his arms. "I have. You lied."

"I didn't know. I swear it." He squinted at her, as if straining to see what wasn't visible.

She wavered, uncertain. Didn't he understand that was what hurt the most? She would never stop loving him, but how could she ever know again for sure if he was telling her the truth? "There isn't anything else to say, so you might as well leave."

"No," he said with deadly calm. "Not yet."

She shot a look back at him, not believing he could be so stubborn, imagining what everyone's reaction would be when they saw him. "You can't stay."

"Sure I can. I was invited."

She cast a glance at his formal clothes. "That was before—when you were pretending."

"I was never pretending," he said quietly.

She drew a hard breath, realizing he had more chance of reaching her with this soft tone than a harsh one. "Just leave," she countered. "You have no right to be here."

"The invitation I got this morning says I do."

Her head snapped up. "You got an— From whom? Trish?"

"From your father."

She was stunned. "My father invited you?"

"Yeah." His mouth curved in that slow-forming grin that had always unnerved her.

He looked suddenly more confident, more sure of himself. That scared her—she knew too well how strong-willed he was, how weak she could be with him.

"Your father called me and invited me this morning."

Of course he would have done that, she realized. Her father had thought she loved Jack. He had done what he'd thought would make her happy. But everything was different now, she reminded herself. "Do what you want," she said turning away quickly. She didn't want to talk to him anymore. She couldn't, she realized, or she would give in to her need to touch him, to hold him. She couldn't let her emotions rule her. Only a fool did that. As she rushed back toward the house, she heard his footsteps behind her.

The cake, still outside the kitchen door, prevented her from entering. As the caterer instructed his men to back up again with the cake, Gwen stepped toward the bushes to give them space. Breathing heavily, she barely heard a soft, "Psst," behind her.

Frowning, she swung around to see Fred pop up from behind a bush. "What are you doing here?"

Puffing out his chest, Fred came to attention. "She isn't married to him yet. And she isn't going to be."

Out of her side vision, she saw Jack had stopped a few feet from them. "You can't stop the wedding."

"Sure, I can. I've made a decision," he declared in an irrevocable tone. "I'm going to kidnap her."

Gwen nearly groaned aloud. "You can't do that."

"I have to make her listen," he said desperately. "None of this was my fault."

Gwen tilted her head, trying to force herself to concentrate on him and not Jack. "You're not innocent. You did go to some party with another woman."

"Give him a chance," Jack said, stepping closer. "He might have had a good reason. Did you?"

"Yeah—well, sort of. I was stupid," he appealed, looking at Jack, "or I'd never have taken Kelsey Haviland to the party."

"Hey, I understand," Jack said with an abundance of man-to-man understanding.

"I don't," Gwen countered, riled by his interference. "You took her to your apartment, too," she reminded Fred.

"I didn't," Fred insisted, raising his hands in surrender. "I swear I didn't bring her to my apartment. I was—was—"

"Framed?" Jack asked, supplying the key word.

Gwen shot him a withering look.

"Yeah, that's what happened. I took her home and went alone to my place. Then I called Trish. I told her I was sorry, and she said that she would come over.

Not fifteen minutes later, Kelsey arrived. She started peeling off her clothes. I couldn't get her to stop...to leave." He flushed with youthful embarrassment despite the fury in his voice. "And then Trish arrived. I didn't understand what had happened," he said, looking perplexed.

"Sounds pretty much like a setup to me," Jack said. "Don't you think so?"

Gwen had to admit it did sound that way.

"So I called Kelsey again," Fred went on. "And she finally admitted that Wesley put her up to it."

"Wesley?" Gwen asked.

"Wesley," he repeated.

Time was vital, Gwen realized as guests began to arrive. "Wait here."

"He'll be here," Jack assured her. "Me, too."

Lifting the skirt of her dress, she rushed back through the house. If he thought she was going to forget everything he'd done because he was offering his help now, he was badly mistaken.

She reached the foyer, wondering how to separate Trish from her giddy-with-joy bridesmaids. The problem quickly took care of itself.

One of the bridesmaids, dressed in a gown a shade paler than Gwen's, descended the stairs. "We're on our way to the photographer for stills," the tall blonde said.

Gwen shot her a token smile, then turned to rush up the stairs but was stopped abruptly by the sight of her father.

"You look lovely," he said, as he approached her from his study.

Gwen mustered another smile and stuck out a sneaker toe from beneath the scalloped hemline of the dress. "The shoes aren't here yet." As he smiled, she stepped forward to adjust his satin, striped ascot. "You look very handsome."

His attention shifted as the wind ruffled the white linen tablecloths and sent one flying. "It's going to storm."

"Quite possibly," she said, thinking of Jack's earlier words about him. "Why did you invite Jack?"

He tucked her arm in his and urged her to walk with him to the opened terrace doors. "I called him this morning to thank him and invited him then."

Gwen lowered her head and set a hand against her billowing skirt. "I didn't want to see him again."

"Don't be too hard on him," he said firmly, frowning at the men struggling to set an elegant ice sculpture on the long buffet table already laden with silver trays of flute champagne glasses. "This is turning into a gastronomic overindulgence, isn't it?" he said critically. "I should have never given your aunt such a free hand."

Gwen looked up with a wan smile.

Placing a fingertip beneath her chin, her father forced her to meet his stare. "Gwen, I was aware of the informant. I knew they had someone in Farrow's organization whom they could rely on for information."

Shock rippled through her. "You knew?" She pulled back instinctively. "You allowed the police to use us?"

"Me," he countered, "Use me." His eyes clouded with concern at her abrupt movement. "I would never have agreed if they hadn't promised personal protection for you and Trish."

"So everyone knew but us?" she asked demandingly.

"I doubt anyone knew before it happened except Captain Caulder, his informant and myself. Jack didn't know," he assured her. "If too many people had been filled in, the plan might not have worked."

Gwen slumped against the opened door. *Jack hadn't known.*

"There's something else."

She tried to shake away the muddled thoughts in her head to concentrate on what he seemed compelled to tell her.

"Your aunt—" He paused and lowered his voice, aware of the ushers nearby dressed in cutaways and silk ascots. "It seems your aunt has been up to some of her shenanigans again. She spoke to Jack and flashed a sizable check at him early this morning. Money to leave you alone. He told her he knew a good charity that would appreciate her generous donation." He chuckled, obviously pleased. "From what I've heard, he sounds like an extremely honest man."

"Honest? Yes," she answered weakly, distantly, then regained her focus, remembering Fred. "I have to go. But answer one question. Do you know Kelsey Haviland?"

His expression instantly turned to disdain, clinching everything for her.

\* \* \*

As she hurried from her father toward her sister's room, his words lingered. Jack hadn't known. He'd been telling the truth, and she hadn't listened. Why hadn't she? she wondered as she opened the door to Trish's bedroom. "Oh, you look beautiful," she said, overlooking her sister's red and puffy eyes.

Nervously, Trish ran a hand across her stomach and the lace that covered the bodice of the high-necked gown and sniffled.

"I've talked to Fred, Trish, and—" Gwen was cut short.

Wildly Trish shook her head, nearly toppling her headpiece. Her hand flew to secure it at a lopsided tilt on her head. "I don't want to hear what he said."

"Yes, you do," Gwen insisted. "You know how much I've been hurt by the men who used me to build their careers. I don't want you to make the biggest mistake of all and marry someone like that."

"Wesley wouldn't do that. He's successful," Trish countered quickly.

Gwen moved to the bed to sit beside her. "At some time you have to be honest with yourself. Don't be a fool," she said softly. "If you really love someone, nothing stands in the way. Nothing."

Trish looked up, startled. "But what he did—"

"Fred didn't do anything, Trish, not really. He was manipulated. He didn't know—" She paused and took a deep breath thinking of what her father had said to her. "He was used," she said, with a calm she hadn't felt in hours. "The woman was Bronte's second cousin."

Trish's eyes widened to saucers.

"Uh-huh," Gwen answered her sister's unspoken question. "It seems Wesley convinced her to make a play for Fred, and Fred—" Gwen shrugged and then repeated Fred's story.

By the time she'd finished, she could tell she'd finally gotten through. "Poor Fred. He didn't know what was happening until it was too late." Gwen smiled wanly in response to her own words. "He had a half-naked woman at his apartment and didn't know how to get rid of her," she added.

For the first time in days, Trish giggled. "I *do* love him."

Gwen felt her own humor returning. "Then go talk to him, Trish. Don't let pride get in the way."

"But all the plans," her sister started. "It's too late, isn't it?"

"It's never too late," Gwen insisted, determined to follow her own advice later. "Come on. We'll sneak down the servants' stairway." Gwen snagged her sister's arm and tugged her toward the door. "If you don't hurry—" As she opened the door, her words were lost to the lilting strains of a violin.

Behind her, Trish balked. Suddenly, panic edged her voice. "Gwen, I can't do this."

Gwen sighed and released her hold on her sister's arm. Trish remained frozen in the doorway. Gwen was at a loss. She couldn't force her sister to find the courage to fight for her love. Trish had to want it for herself. There was nothing left for her to do but resign herself to having given her best efforts. "I'll tell him to leave then."

Disturbed, she wandered downstairs and outside. Guests waited. Music had begun. She couldn't blame Trish for her reluctance to make more of a fool of herself.

Gwen wove her way past late-coming guests. Side-stepping to avoid the loquacious Bronte, she scurried toward the bushes near the front of the house to find Fred, praying Jack hadn't left. He'd said everyone was allowed to play the fool three times. She hoped that he really believed it.

Then she saw them. They stood huddled like conspirators. Looking crestfallen that Gwen was alone, Fred voiced his fears dully. "She said no?"

Gwen tried to soften the news. "I thought she was coming down. Fred—"

But he was looking past Gwen, rearing back slightly as if something frightening lurked behind her.

At Jack's frown, Gwen glanced over her left shoulder. A formidable opponent was charging up the incline.

"What are you doing here?" Ardelle demanded, her heels clicking quick and short. She bridged the remaining distance between them in three unladylike strides. "He shouldn't be here." She appealed to Gwen as if she were a genie with the power to make Fred disappear.

"Yes, he should." The voice came from the right of Gwen—soft, firm, feminine.

Fred lighted up. "Trish," he murmured, his face widening into a smile.

Gwen felt as if she were standing in the eye of a gathering storm.

Panic rushed into Ardelle's voice. "Trish, what are you doing down here? You're supposed to be in the foyer."

Joan of Arc couldn't have looked braver. Straightening her back, Trish shook her head. "I'm not marrying him."

Gwen winced as Ardelle's fingers bit into her arm. "Talk to her," Ardelle insisted low, as if conspiring against the others in the room. "I'll get help."

Trish didn't need any help. She and Fred came together like two magnets. "Oh, Fred, I'm so sorry. I didn't know, you never told me, and—"

"I've been so stupid," he murmured back, his arms wrapped tightly around her.

"No, I have," she answered.

Gwen decided they both had been dumb, but now wasn't the time for condemnations. "You should leave," she urged, breaking into their dreamy state. "Ardelle is getting reinforcements." The reminder jerked them apart. "I'll inform the guests that the wedding has been canceled," Gwen assured them. With a glance toward the murmuring voices at the back of the house, she stepped closer and hugged her sister. "Be happy," she said, then nudged Trish toward Fred.

Looking ready to face invincible forces for love, Trish and Fred linked hands. Then Fred hesitated.

Now what? Gwen wanted to scream as his eyes turned on her for more answers, as if she were wisdom personified.

"I didn't plan very well." Concern edged his voice. "I parked my car outside the gates." Bewilderment furrowed his brow. "I think I need a getaway car."

Gwen wavered between a laugh at his befuddled look and a groan at his dilemma. Was nothing simple? Even if she sprinted up the stairs for her car keys, she would never get back down before Trish and Fred were trapped by Ardelle and a legion of Bowmans.

"Here." Jack jingled his car keys before him. "Take mine."

Fred lurched for the keys, then hooked an arm around Trish's waist.

"The family will never believe this," she said, her soft giggle trailing behind them as she scurried away with Fred toward Jack's car.

Gwen's eyes silently followed them. She held her breath until she saw that Fred had turned the car around. As it sped toward the gates, she sighed in relief at resolving one predicament, then steeled herself to face her own. Her heart pounding, she raised her gaze to look at Jack. "Thank you."

He nodded, but said nothing. An excruciating silence passed. As he stared at her—too familiar, too unwavering—she felt as if someone were strangling her, preventing her from talking. Emotions swarmed in on her. Mostly she ached for him to open his arms to her.

In the distance she heard the buzz of voices from the group gathered for the wedding. But her world had already narrowed to only the space that separated them. "Does it hurt?" she asked with a glance toward the sling.

"Enough." He wouldn't beg. He promised himself that he wouldn't beg.

It wasn't fair for him to look so relaxed, Gwen thought, when nerves were jumping within her. "Shouldn't you be resting?"

He shook his head as if the idea was absurd. "You said you loved me. Do you remember that?" His eyes, as well as his tone, carried a challenge. "Did you lie?"

He captured her eyes with his steadfast stare. Beneath the stormy gray sky, Gwen felt sunshine and warmth. Her heart quickened to a light, fluttery beat. She knew that if she didn't feel his arms around her soon, she'd fall apart and give in to all the emotion she'd held in check for the past twenty-four hours.

"Do you love me?" he repeated, with the annoyed, exhausted flippancy of a man whose earnestness had nearly run out.

Overcome with emotion, Gwen was speechless. Didn't he feel the love she wanted to give to only him? And how could she make him understand that it hadn't been him that she didn't trust? It had been herself. If she'd been honest with herself, she would have realized that sooner. Pride, again, had stood in her way. Always pride. It was because she'd had doubts about her own judgment that she'd expected the worst from him. "I've made plenty of mistakes before—"

He winced and she knew he'd misunderstood her words.

"My father told me everything." She watched a muscle nervously twitching in his jaw and wanted desperately to soothe it into calm beneath her fingertips.

"No, he didn't. Not everything. He didn't know I had planned to tell you about what I'd learned." Clumsy, Jack thought. He was stumbling through the most important moment in his life.

Agitated, he ran a hand through his hair. "I've tried to forget you. I can't. I couldn't stay away. My whole life I've been searching—" He tried to explain. "And...I hadn't realized what I'd really been searching for. But, for too long, I believed love wasn't meant for me." He glanced toward the gathering throng at the back of the house. He couldn't see the champagne glasses or the musicians, but the Ashcroft wealth surrounded him. He grimaced and forced all that still gnawed at him to the surface. "You talk about honesty. Hell, I've been honest. I know I can never offer you the kind of life that you're used to. Your ancestors—your whole family is—"

"Is what?" she interrupted.

He felt heat and saw it in the darkening of her eyes as she stood before him—her fiery hair flying back beneath the rush of wind, her skin golden against the soft peach dress.

"What does it matter who my ancestors were?" she asked, frustrated that they were even discussing such a thing. "I live a life like you do." She closed the distance until only inches separated them. "*You* are a bigger fool than I am. At least I'm honest enough with myself to know I've been stupid and full of pride and wrong about everything except that I love you.''

He warmed at the fiery emotion in her eyes.

''I may be an Ashcroft, but I understand what real—spiritual—wealth is. Do you?''

A wry grin of both amusement and uncertainty curved his lips. As she'd grown stormier, he'd become more calm. ''Yeah, finally,'' he said, tugging her to him. ''Finally, I think I do.''

Her hand touched his chest, then slowly slid upward to coil around his neck.

Jack shook his head. ''I think at times I nearly went crazy because I loved you so much.''

Gwen could hardly breathe he kissed her so hard, his mouth hot and hungry, flaring a fire between them. Love wouldn't elude her this time, she realized.

He laughed softly against her cheek. ''How does a house, a couple of kids and a station wagon sound to you?''

Her arm still snug around his neck, she brushed his ear with a whisper. ''Perfect.''

The sound of Wesley's voice intruding forced her to make her answering kiss quick.

''Where is Trish?'' he bellowed, charging up the slight incline, trailed by Ralston and Ardelle.

''She stood you up, Wesley,'' Gwen informed him with great pleasure.

Ralston's face colored crimson. Beside him, Ardelle turned pale, her shoulders sagging. Wesley blustered out, ''She can't do that.''

"It's too late," Gwen said, stifling a smile. "She already has."

Just in time to contain the budding chaos, Gwen's father stepped forward from the sidelines with the well-trained diplomacy and persuasiveness of a corporate lawyer. Though his expression remained deadly serious, Gwen noted the sparkle in his eyes. Taking charge, he offered consoling words to Wesley while leading him back toward the guests.

"How could she do this to us?" Ardelle ranted. "Do you know what everyone will say? Why we'll be—" Her words stopped suddenly. Her mouth hanging open, she stared with widening eyes at the hand Jack had secured on Gwen's waist. "Oh, no," she said on a soft moan, clutching at Ralston's arm for support. "I think I need to lie down," she told her husband.

Gwen managed not to laugh until Ralston had ushered her sister out of hearing range. "Have you any idea what you're getting into? We're a screwy lot."

Jack smiled. "They sound great to me." He turned her in his arms and kissed her again. "I was wrong. Really wrong," he said huskily. "I thought people didn't get what they wanted."

"Some do," she murmured against his lips.

"Yeah, I know. I got you."

She tossed back her head, her smile as bright and eager as ever. "About that boat of yours—" Lightly she ran her fingers down the length of his throat. "We could honeymoon on it."

He chuckled over the pleasure so obvious in her face. "Whatever you want." He tried to memorize the feel of her against him. It wasn't enough. "Let's leave."

Gwen glanced back over her shoulder toward the guests gathered.

He arched a brow. "The champagne isn't flowing yet."

"It will be," she said lightly. "Before the afternoon is over, everyone will get soundly soused in sympathy for Wesley."

Jack shook his head, his eyes smiling at her. "I'm more a beer man myself."

"With chili burgers," she said, expressing her agreement by nibbling at his bottom lip. "Do you know where we can get some?"

His lips curved in a slow enticing smile, then he turned her toward the driveway with him. "My place."

"Exactly where I want to be," she said, smiling up at him. "From now on."

* * * * *

## *Silhouette Special Edition.*

You loved the older sister in
*The Cowboy's Lady*
You adored the younger sister in
*The Sheriff Takes a Wife*
Now get a load of the brothers in
Debbie Macomber's new trilogy.

continuing with May's
tender tale of love for a

# STAND-IN WIFE

When Paul Manning's beloved wife died, he was devastated. But raising three kids alone left little time for healing . . . until his lovely sister-in-law, Leah, appeared and brought calm to his household. At first it was for the children—for the memory of her sister—then . . . gradually, magically, unashamedly . . . for the love of Paul.

Look for the third book of Debbie Macomber's THOSE MANNING MEN in July in your local bookstore.

If you missed the first book of THOSE MANNING MEN, *MARRIAGE OF INCONVENIENCE* (SE#732), order your copy now by sending your name, address, zip or postal code, along with a check or money order (please do not send cash) for $3.39, plus 75¢ for postage and handling ($1.00 in Canada), payable to Silhouette Books to:

| In the U.S. | In Canada |
|---|---|
| 3010 Walden Avenue | P.O. Box 609 |
| P.O. Box 1396 | Fort Erie, Ontario |
| Buffalo, NY 14269-1396 | L2A 5X3 |

Please specify book title with your order.
Canadian residents add applicable federal and provincial taxes.

SEMAN-2

## *Silhouette Special Edition*

### Commencing in May . . .

**The stories of the men and women who ride the range, keep the home fires burning and live to love.**

## *Cowboy Country*

### by Myrna Temte

Where the soul is free and the heart unbound . . . and the good guys still win. Don't miss *For Pete's Sake,* #739, the first of three stories rustled up with love from Silhouette Special Edition.

SEDAW-1

## "GET AWAY FROM IT ALL" SWEEPSTAKES

# HERE'S HOW THE SWEEPSTAKES WORKS

### NO PURCHASE NECESSARY

To enter each drawing, complete the appropriate Official Entry Form or a 3" by 5" index card by hand-printing your name, address and phone number and the trip destination that the entry is being submitted for (i.e., Caneel Bay, Canyon Ranch or London and the English Countryside) and mailing it to: Get Away From It All Sweepstakes, P.O. Box 1397, Buffalo, New York 14269-1397.

No responsibility is assumed for lost, late or misdirected mail. Entries must be sent separately with first class postage affixed, and be received by: 4/15/92 for the Caneel Bay Vacation Drawing, 5/15/92 for the Canyon Ranch Vacation Drawing and 6/15/92 for the London and the English Countryside Vacation Drawing. Sweepstakes is open to residents of the U.S. (except Puerto Rico) and Canada, 21 years of age or older as of 5/31/92.

For complete rules send a self-addressed, stamped (WA residents need not affix return postage) envelope to: Get Away From It All Sweepstakes, P.O. Box 4892, Blair, NE 68009.

© 1992 HARLEQUIN ENTERPRISES LTD.                                   SWP-RL3

---

## "GET AWAY FROM IT ALL" SWEEPSTAKES

# HERE'S HOW THE SWEEPSTAKES WORKS

### NO PURCHASE NECESSARY

To enter each drawing, complete the appropriate Official Entry Form or a 3" by 5" index card by hand-printing your name, address and phone number and the trip destination that the entry is being submitted for (i.e., Caneel Bay, Canyon Ranch or London and the English Countryside) and mailing it to: Get Away From It All Sweepstakes, P.O. Box 1397, Buffalo, New York 14269-1397.

No responsibility is assumed for lost, late or misdirected mail. Entries must be sent separately with first class postage affixed, and be received by: 4/15/92 for the Caneel Bay Vacation Drawing, 5/15/92 for the Canyon Ranch Vacation Drawing and 6/15/92 for the London and the English Countryside Vacation Drawing. Sweepstakes is open to residents of the U.S. (except Puerto Rico) and Canada, 21 years of age or older as of 5/31/92.

For complete rules send a self-addressed, stamped (WA residents need not affix return postage) envelope to: Get Away From It All Sweepstakes, P.O. Box 4892, Blair, NE 68009.

© 1992 HARLEQUIN ENTERPRISES LTD.                                   SWP-RLS

# "GET AWAY FROM IT ALL"

## Brand-new Subscribers-Only Sweepstakes

# OFFICIAL ENTRY FORM

This entry must be received by: April 15, 1992
This month's winner will be notified by: April 30, 1992
Trip must be taken between: May 31, 1992—May 31, 1993

**YES,** I want to win the Caneel Bay Plantation vacation for
two. I understand the prize includes round-trip airfare and the
two additional prizes revealed in the BONUS PRIZES insert.

Name _____

Address _____

City _____

State/Prov._____ Zip/Postal Code_____

Daytime phone number_____
(Area Code)

Return entries with invoice in envelope provided. Each book in this shipment has two
entry coupons — and the more coupons you enter, the better your chances of winning!
© 1992 HARLEQUIN ENTERPRISES LTD.                            1M-CPN

---

# "GET AWAY FROM IT ALL"

## Brand-new Subscribers-Only Sweepstakes

# OFFICIAL ENTRY FORM

This entry must be received by: April 15, 1992
This month's winner will be notified by: April 30, 1992
Trip must be taken between: May 31, 1992—May 31, 1993

**YES,** I want to win the Caneel Bay Plantation vacation for
two. I understand the prize includes round-trip airfare and the
two additional prizes revealed in the BONUS PRIZES insert.

Name _____

Address _____

City _____

State/Prov._____ Zip/Postal Code_____

Daytime phone number_____
(Area Code)

Return entries with invoice in envelope provided. Each book in this shipment has two
entry coupons — and the more coupons you enter, the better your chances of winning!
© 1992 HARLEQUIN ENTERPRISES LTD.                            1M-CPN